The 2017 Anthology of Winning Irish Short Stories

THREE
SISTERS
PRESS

The Ireland's Own 2017 Anthology of Winning Short Stories

Editor: Phil Murphy

Production Editor: Helen Ashdown

Design: Rosbui Media, Co. Wexford

Published by: Three Sisters Press Ltd. Co. Wexford

Printed by: Swiftprint Solutions Ltd. Rathnew, Co. Wicklow

Distribution by: Gill Distribution, Hume Avenue, Park West, Dublin 12

© Copyright 2017, Ireland's Own, Channing House, Rowe Street, Wexford

ISBN: 978-0-9573162-9-4

Disclaimer:

While best efforts have been used in preparing this book, the author and publisher make no representations or warranties of any kind and assume no liabilities of any kind with respect to the accuracy or complete-ness of the contents and specifically disclaim any implied warranties of merchantability or fitness of use for a particular purpose. Neither the author nor the publisher shall be held liable or responsible to any person or entity with respect to any loss or incidental or consequential damages caused, or alleged to have been caused, directly or indirectly, by the information contained herein.

What They Said About Us

Quotes from the forewords to our previous Anthologies.

"IRELAND'S OWN has been like a good kindly Fairy Godmother for all of us, publishing our first works, giving us encouragement ... the magazine has been like a friend, a great cushion against the tough world out there"
– *Maeve Binchy, 2010*

"MY LINKS with *Ireland's Own* began in far-off days in my home town of Doneraile, Co. Cork, where I first encountered this fountain of stories, essays, jokes and Irishness in Titridge's shop. It has continued right through my life ... my last moments awake each night are spent reading the *Ireland's Own*"
– *Donncha Ó Dúlaing, 2011*

"I COMMEND *Ireland's Own* for their continued support and commitment to new Irish writers. Telling stories is in our lifeblood. The tradition of the seanachai is ingrained in us and it is why we have so many wonderful writers in every genre"
– *Patricia Scanlan, 2012*

"HUGE THANKS to the wonderful team at *Ireland's Own* for your continued support and encouragement to writers everywhere. You've no idea how much it means and long may your magical tradition of storytelling continue. It's a truly

amazing thing, actually seeing something you've written there in black and white taking its first baby steps out into the world"
– *Claudia Carroll, 2013*

"WHEN I had my first manuscript accepted by a publisher, I danced around the kitchen and sang 'Alleluia'. We writers have a deep desire to see our name [and our work] in print. This Anthology provides that opportunity. Congratulations to all whose stories are glowing within"
– *Alice Taylor, 2014*

"THERE'S *Ireland's Own*, one of the most widely read journals in this hemisphere, which mercifully provides outlets for all sorts of writing: from the comic to the ironic to the tragic, from reality to fiction … To know the magazine is still there is comforting to say the least"
– *Billy Roche, 2015*

"I AM delighted to be involved with the *Ireland's Own* annual Anthology. Storytelling is something we do when we are grieving, or when we are full of joy ... It is all storytelling. And it is what makes us human. *Ireland's Own* has been celebrating and encouraging the art of storytelling for over a century"
– *Michael Harding, 2016*

Introduction

IRELAND'S OWN in conjunction with publishers Three Sisters Press, is very pleased to bring to readers our 8th anthology of the winners and other highly commended entries in the long-running annual writing competitions run through the magazine.

This book is compiled from the 500 plus entries we received for our 2016 writing competitions and we are satisfied that the content is once again of a very good standard, indicative of the great writing talent out there.

Ireland's Own receives a great many submissions from our regular contributors every year, and we also receive a large number of unsolicited contributions every week, many of them of a good quality. We are only able to use a small portion of all these, but we do try to be encouraging and sympathetic in our approach as we are conscious of the great desire among people out there to get their work into print, and the small number of potential outlets available to them.

The anthology and our writing competitions are an essential part of that policy of encouragement and support. We thank former *Ireland's Own* editors, Gerry Breen, Margaret Galvin and Phil Murphy for their continued involvement with this worthwhile project.

We wish all the contributors future success if you continue to pursue your writing ambitions; *Ireland's Own* is very happy to have helped you take these first steps along the road.

The short stories and memoirs in this publication offer a good flavour of what is available every week in *Ireland's Own*, the publishing phenomenon that has continued without a break since 1902.

Our unique mix of entertaining, educational and informative features, song words, jokes, cookery, lifestyle and health, history and personal memoirs, also includes our old friends such as Cassidy,

Miss Flanagan and Dan Conway, and a substantial section specially for younger readers,

Even after 115 years the old maxim about *Ireland's Own* is as true as ever, The Week Wouldn't Be The Same Without It! And perhaps we can now say that the year would not be the same without the annual *Ireland's Own Anthology* of short stories and memories.

Sean Nolan, Editor, *Ireland's Own* and
Shea Tomkins, Assistant Editor, *Ireland's Own*

Contacting *Ireland's Own*

You can check out *Ireland's Own*, sample what we have to offer, take out subscriptions and air your views on our lively website at *www.irelandsown.ie*.

Phone us at 053 91 40140. If dialling from overseas the number to ring is 00353 5391 40140.

Email articles to be considered for publication to: *submissions@ irelandsown.ie*

For general enquiries, email: *info@irelandsown.ie*

For subscriptions: *iosubs@irelandsown.ie*

You may write to us at *Ireland's Own*, Channing House, Rowe Street, Wexford, Ireland.

Editor's Note

AS A RETIRED editor of *Ireland's Own* I am very happy to maintain my association with the magazine as compiler and editor of the yearly anthologies.

I congratulate all those who appear in this year's production; quite a few regulars are again included, but others are being published in a book for the first time and their appearance in this volume will certainly mean a great deal to them, in particular.

I thank you all for your help and co-operation with this, our eighth annual anthology, and I hope you feel pleased and happy with the end result.

The adjudicators assure me the standard was very high once again and it should be a source of much satisfaction and pride to have made it between these covers.

The popularity of our writing competitions and the Anthology itself continues to grow and this volume contains entries from sixteen Irish counties, Britain, Jersey in the Channel Islands and Colorado in the USA.

Well done also to the hundreds of others who entered our long-running annual writing competitions. I would certainly encourage you to stick with your writing; I am sure you will find it stimulating and personally rewarding and perhaps your turn will come in future anthologies.

A special word of thanks to Billy Keane, author and columnist, and son of the legendary writer and playwright, John B. Keane, for providing a foreword for this year's edition; his support and encouragement is greatly appreciated by us, and also by all the writers.

He follows in a distinguished line of people who have endorsed our efforts over the years, including the late Maeve Binchy, Donncha Ó

Dúlaing, Patricia Scanlan, Claudia Carroll, Alice Taylor, Billy Roche and Michael Harding.

My thanks to friends and former colleagues, *Ireland's Own* editors Sean Nolan and Shea Tomkins, for their ongoing help and support, and to the efficient *Ireland's Own* staff who administer the competitions and book sales, and keep the wheels turning so well throughout the year.

I acknowledge the help and co-operation of Michael Freeman and all at Three Sisters Press, publishers of this edition of the *Ireland's Own Anthology of Winning Short Stories*, Rosbui Media for design and lay-out and the many others involved behind the scenes.

Phil Murphy
September 2017

Foreword

By Billy Keane
Columnist, author, publican
son of legendary playwright, John B. Keane

I RELAND'S OWN is just that. Most of us who read and love the old magazine feel a sense of ownership; *Ireland's Own* is Ireland's very Own.

The short story has long been championed by this magazine. It was often the last refuge of the short story in times when most other publications felt the medium was old-fashioned.

The short stories and memoirs in this anthology follow on in a noble tradition – we are a nation of story tellers and talkers. There's plenty of material out there if you know where to look and listen.

An example: this lad came into the bar just last night, and he wasn't there for a drink but to put some money in the St Anthony alms box, it being a well-known fact the saint is very good at finding the lost. It wasn't so much that the man lost the money, but more of a case that he hid it after a few drinks in a place he was sure would not be discovered by his beloved, who was very much given to the purchase of ornaments and mugs with floral designs.

We asked him if he searched in the usual places like the toilet cistern, under the mattress and his pockets. He replied in the affirmative and after a sigh he declared 'I searched everywhere, even behind the wall paper.'

My Dad had his first piece published in *Ireland's Own* and he told me the recognition gave him great confidence. There was also a small cheque he said, but more likely a postal order in those days, which was a big deal for a small boy, and was the first money dad ever earned as a writer.

Ireland's Own publishes amateur writers every week all year round, and an anthology of the best entries to their annual writing competitions every year around now. This is public service publishing at its finest. Keep on going *Ireland's Own*. You have done us all some service since 1902. There is such enduring quality in *Ireland's Own* and so many 'I wish I wrote that one' short stories.

The short story is back in the big time. The beauty of the short story, from the writer's point of view, is the end is nigh. There's finality. A novel can take years to write, and then it might not be much good at the end of all that torture. Get writing, and if you've written one, well then you might as well write another.

Here's a tip for you – read just one story a night. That way you will make this wonderful collection 'far to go.' And your mind will not be clogged up with different themes and stories.

My mother booked *Ireland's Own* every week, and then when she was finished reading it from cover to cover, under the covers, she posted the magazine off to my Aunt Chris in The Bronx. This is something that is repeated all over the country. For many emigrants, the *Ireland's Own* is like a letter from home.

So this year I will keep up the tradition and send these wonderful stories to New York. There's continuity in these pages and a loyalty to both the reader and the writer that has passed the toughest test of all in publishing, and that is the test of time itself.

I was so honoured to be asked to write this foreword. We are nearly 80 years on from Dad's first lines in *Ireland's Own*, where careers begin at every age, and the love of the word will never end.

Billy Keane
September, 2017

BILLY KEANE has been a regular columnist with The *Irish Independent* for nearly a decade and a half, commenting on all the big sporting occasions and on life in general, usually laced with humour but sometimes with an acerbic edge. In November 2016 he published a collection of those columns under the title *The Best of Billy Keane – From a Writer Who Sees Extraordinary Deeds in Day-to-Day Living*.

He has written novels, including *The Last of The Heroes* and *The Ballad of Mo and G*. He co-wrote *Rucks Mauls and Gaelic Footballs* with Irish rugby international, Moss Keane, and ghosted the autobiography of Billy Morgan, Cork Gaelic football legend, entitled *Rebel Rebel*.

Billy is son of writer, John B. Keane, author of a large number of much loved classic Irish plays, and he runs the family pub in Listowel, made famous by his late father and mother.

Contents

Highly Commended

Dirty Silver on the Matt Black Rock

By Niamh MacCabe,
Fivemilebourne, Co. Leitrim

A young couple are on an idyllic day out, heading for a rock pool on the edge of the Caribbean that only the locals know about, the ocean shimmering ahead of them. It reminds her of a boreen back home in Connemara. It almost seems too good to be true.

I AM BESIDE my beloved, nothing matters. I watch him while he drives, his arm hanging out of the window, catching the odd flower-head that appears between the rocks as we pass. He offers his catches to me and I place them with ceremony on the dusty dashboard where they shine, jiggle, and wilt faster than they can be replaced.

He is whistling and I am listening to the tuneful sound of brittle little stones splitting and crunching beneath the hot tyres. An ocean shimmer sighs ahead, brimming with promise.

We are heading for the rock pool down the little cul-de-sac zigzagging to the sea, a stretch known only to locals. I could almost be back home, on some narrow Irish boreen etched into the rock of Connemara, if it wasn't for the Caribbean sun radiating off the roadside boulders, and the scent of boundless growth.

Everton breaks into song, some nonsensical sea shanty. A tune-less singer, he belts out songs with passion, presuming to

1

make up for his lack through volume. I laugh, and turn towards the road in front. Another car has come into view, advancing slowly towards us along the narrow track.

An indistinct reggae baseline becomes louder as the car approaches, threatening to drown out Everton's ditty. Undeterred, he weaves his patchy song into the fabric of the encroaching beat and thus his little melody survives. It is a perfect soundtrack to our morning, elemental, sensual. I clap and swoon in mock ecstasy, my hand-clap slowing down to blend with the deep throb as it draws closer.

The two cars meet. As we pull in to let it pass, the base of the reggae drone abstracts and begins to reverberate wildly off the boulders. Discordant sounds echo, splintering into deafening booms, a deconstructed parody of music. The glowering youths edge past slowly, their aggression resonating in the skewed rhythm. They come to an abrupt stop, hemming us in.

There have been attacks on tourists, increasing in severity in the last few years. These have culminated in several murders as some of the local population retaliate against the influx of wealthy whites who use the island as their playground, cordoning off the beauty spots for themselves and leaving the disenfranchised local youths to grapple with the notion that life has not been fair to them.

Two cars, side by side, cradled in menace, hot engines idling. Everton, a native of the island, challenges the threat with a greeting spoken in the local dialect. The malevolent spell seems to break. The car revs high and speeds off, scattering pebbles in its wake.

Shaken, we laugh, hearing the isolated tendrils of sound reform into a reggae weave as it recedes into the past. We swing our car back onto the track and continue our trip down to the edge of the ocean. The tilted day is back on its axis.

At road's end, we park, and hop across the boulders until we come upon it – a deep, glimmering pool carved out of the ancient rock by a temperamental sea. Today the sea lies idly by, down a small cliff face. It grouses, and spits tatters of foam up, warning us not to sink into a slumbering sense of well-being.

The still pool is bordered on all sides by pock-marked, sharp, volcanic rock which seems to hold a memory of its violent past. Despite the serene setting, the beautiful black rock is capable of inflicting a deep cut on those who become complacent.

We strip. Throwing our belongings onto the hot rocks, I hear a sharp clang. He answers my look.

'I brought a knife.'

'What the hell? A knife? Ya expectin' to grapple with Jaws?'

'I just did.'

The previous evening, Everton's grandmother watched him read my fate through her set of Tarot cards, something neither of us took seriously though the reading was ominous. But Mima did not dismiss it. This morning, before we set out, she pleaded with her grandson not to venture away from home today.

He laughed off her warnings, but his superstitious self got the better of him. He brought along a hunting knife, a terrifying thing, which he hid from me, rightly fearing ridicule. Now it lies exposed, dirty silver on the matt black rock, the clang of its metal resounding around us.

'Ya flippin' eejit.'

He laughs. Jumping into the pool's still water, he tries to repeat the words. A familiar sparring match begins, him imitating my dialect and me imitating his. I stand at the edge of the pool.

I am the first to see them. Hat pulled down tight, face covered with a bandana, someone is hopping over the rocks towards our pool. Another follows behind, also wearing the face covering, a slit between the hat and bandana for his eyes. Both of them are heading directly for me.

The words gush out, my mouth struggling to shape the sounds.

'There's guys coming! They're running! There's two guys running!'

I see the guns. I think of my nakedness, the sharp rocks.

Everton roars.

'Get down! Get your clothes!'

He hauls himself out of the pool, grabs for the knife. The young hooded men have nearly reached us and, with handguns pointed on outstretched arms, begin yelling muffled orders at us not to move.

I stand staring, open-mouthed. Everton jumps in front of me and shouts that he is local, where he lives, who his family are. Despite his efforts at bravado, his breaking voice betrays fear.

One points his gun at me, the other holds his gun stiffly in both hands, aiming at Everton who flails his arms, knife gripped in one hand, bellowing at them to get back, get the hell away from us. They watch, then tell him to throw his knife over the cliff edge behind us into the sea. Everton shouts louder, stabbing the air between us and them, his vulnerability stoking an unfamiliar violence in him.

'Throw your knife in the water. I'll count to three. If you don't, I'll shoot you', one of them says.

Everton curses, spits, takes a decisive step forward, waves his knife in their direction.

Their countdown begins, steady, confident.

'Throw it!' I shout.

Everton stops, looks at our attackers. All four of us hold breath. The sea lashes a mockery against the cliff face below.

He flings it behind him in an arc, letting out a wild cry of despair as the knife flies from his grip towards the sea. It hits off the cliff face with several loud clangs, followed by a distant splash as it falls into the water below.

Silence follows. I hold the stare of the man closest to me. My body begins to shake.

'You'll be hurt,' I tell myself, 'you'll be cut, the rocks are sharp, stay alive.'

Everton takes a step back to stand alongside me, reaching over to my quaking shoulders. The man jabs the air with his gun.

'Don't move! I told you! Put your hands down!'

I can hear the swell of the sea below, thrashing at the cliff face. I think of the tarnished silver knife swirling gracefully down through the water, coming to rest on a soft sea floor, silent, still, beneath the turbulent surface.

They step backwards to our belongings, eyes and guns still trained on us. One ransacks while the other keeps watch.

I catch Everton's whisper.

'We'll jump.'

'What?'

'We'll jump into the sea.'

'What? No! I can't!'

'We have to. I'll count to three. We'll turn, run to the edge, and jump.'

It is a steep drop of about ten metres into deep unpredictable water, but it is escape. I know it is our only chance. I know I have to do it. I don't know if I can.

'One. Two. Three!'

We turn. I am a blind heartbeat behind him. I am his shadow. I cling to his faith in me, afraid to let go, terrified of going.

I scramble after him, away from the pool, over the volcanic black rock, the short distance to the cliff brink. A sharp edge tears my calf open on the way. I hear the men roar.

We reach the brink. Everton jumps.

A hovering bird of prey with his arms outstretched and his head facing down, I watch his body disappear in front of me. I hear the outraged hollering behind me. I hear him hit the water below.

I am alone. The sea, the edge, the sky above, all watching, all waiting, all one beat away from me.

It seems to take forever to fall. When I hit the sea, I feel pain streak through my torn calf. I sink down into cold, and pirouette in the depths until I can distinguish the glistening light of the top from the murky dark of the bottom. I twist my body upwards and rise.

When I surface, I am facing the cliff I have flung myself from. I see the two men, standing where I stood. They are baying with rage, guns pointing at me. The waves are high, I cannot see Everton. I turn and dive underwater, breaking the surface some metres out. Without looking back, I swim away from the cliff.

Adrenaline hoisting me above the manic pull of the ocean, I prepare for a bullet between the shoulder blades. I imagine the pain will be short and hot, and am grateful for the cover the rough sea provides. The water swirls around me, mirroring my panic. I see my own blood in the waves, my leg wound bleeding. I think of sharks.

The shouting behind me has stopped, or maybe I can't hear them above the sound of the ocean. I see a promontory ahead. I know that I have to make it there. I begin to intone 'swim swim swim' and push through wave after battering wave into the open sea.

Between the swells, I see Everton close by. We swim steadily without exchanging a glance, for no comfort can be found but on dry land, and though it is a shared goal, our journeys there are singular in purpose.

We reach the promontory, exhausted, numb. Pulling each other up, we clamber into the nearest crevice. We huddle together, clinging to the black rocks at the water's edge. I hide my face in my hands and weep, Everton is silent, both of us trapped raw in our own anguish.

There we wait. Buffeted by errant waves, we watch the tide rise before us. It creeps up the promontory, covering one by one the sharp black rocks, their violent volcanic past memorised deep within them.

Niamh MacCabe was born in Dublin, grew up in Paris, in north-west Ireland, and in Washington DC, where she graduated as a visual artist from the Corcoran School of Art. She worked overseas in the animated film industry, returning to Ireland to raise her children. She began writing in 2014 and has had a great deal of success in a short time, winning in 2016 alone the Molly Keane Creative Writing Award, The Wasafiri New Writing Prize, The Short Story Competition and the Ireland's Own *Writing Competition.*

Easy and Slow

By Alyson Meadowcroft,
St. Helier, Jersey, Channel Islands

I was put in charge of Uncle Billy's latest greyhound purchase;
he was a lovely looking dog and we became firm friends. There was
just one snag … he was no good at running.

MY UNCLE BILLY used to keep greyhounds for racing, and I helped him. This meant that I fed them, groomed them and took them out on their training runs. I loved every minute of it. People think greyhounds aren't good pets, that they're only for racing, but they're wrong! Every one of Uncle Billy's dogs was a character in their own right. This is the story of one of them called Easy and Slow, who was very special.

It all happened in Belfast about fifty years ago. I was 14 and still at school with the Brothers at the bottom of the Falls Road. Every day after school I used to head off to Bryson Street, to give Uncle Billy a hand with the dogs. One afternoon in April, I arrived as usual at four o' clock.

Uncle Billy was waiting for me with a look of excitement on his face. 'Bobby lad, come on in, I've got a new dog to show you,' says he. I followed him into the kitchen.

There, lying on a mat by the stove, was the loveliest greyhound I'd ever seen, with a beautiful tan coat and white markings on its face. As we came in, it stood up and stretched itself. It was the size of a wee donkey, with legs that didn't stop at its haunches.

8

Uncle Billy took hold of its collar and said, 'This boy is going to be a real winner, Bobby; got him from that farmer in Dungannon. He has a dead-on pedigree and we can't lose.'

I stroked the dog which nuzzled my hand and sniffed me carefully. His nose felt like velvet. 'What's his name, Uncle Billy?' I asked.

'A real good one, Bobby. He's called Easy and Slow, and you are going to have special responsibility for him!' he replied, with a knowing smile in his eyes.

From that day on I was hooked on Easy and Slow. We became great friends. I spent all my spare time with him. Every evening after school, he was waiting for me. I groomed him until he shone like silk. I even cleaned his teeth and his claws. He was a real picture when I put on his muzzle and lead, and headed for the Falls Park to walk him. I even started calling in before school each morning to give him his breakfast.

But there was one problem. Nice as he was, Easy and Slow couldn't run! We soon discovered that when we took him out to the country for training. No matter what we did, the dog couldn't get any speed up. I even tried running beside him, to encourage him, but he couldn't keep up with me. We brought out one of the other dogs but it was no use. Easy and Slow just didn't have the makings of a champion.

Uncle Billy was heartbroken. All he could think about was the waste of money. He said the only solution was to sell Easy and Slow to some other unsuspecting punter. That didn't please me, I was so fond of the dog by now that I felt I couldn't part with him.

My uncle decided to wait for an easy race at Celtic Park, enter Easy and Slow and get a couple of prospective buyers along to watch. Hopefully he would make a half decent show of himself.

Anyway, I was left to look after Easy and Slow and we had some good times together. He had a lovely personality and I enjoyed all the time I spent with him. But it all came to a head one cold afternoon in October.

'Easy' and I had been up at the Park for our usual run, and Auntie Kathleen had lunch ready when we came back. Uncle Billy had been away all morning and wasn't back by the time we sat down to eat. Auntie Kathleen was a great cook and we had ribs, cabbage and big floury Comber spuds that melted in your mouth. She left Uncle Billy's plate on the stove to keep warm, but there was no sign of him by the time we finished.

Not wanting to waste good food, she offered it to me. I cleared the ribs and gave 'Easy' the cabbage and spuds. You should have seen the look on his face, he wolfed them down in two minutes flat and then lay down on his blanket by the fire for a snooze.

About half an hour later, who arrives home but Uncle Billy! He wasn't worried about missing his lunch, he was full of the news he had. 'Easy' was entered in the half mile race at Celtic Park that evening, and two fellas from Dublin were coming to watch him. If he managed to finish, they were going to buy him!

Well, I didn't half start to sweat. A dog's supposed to be starved before a race, not full of cabbage and spuds. 'Easy' had enough problems without me adding to them.

Uncle Billy told me I would be in charge of Easy tonight, putting him in the trap and getting him set up. What could I do? I decided the best thing was to keep my mouth shut and hope for the best. But by the time we had reached Celtic Park, I had almost lost my nerve.

Uncle Billy introduced me to the prospective buyers and cast a last eye over 'Easy'. He looked a cracker. I had spent ages on grooming him and his tan hide shone like leather. His ears were pricked up and he quivered with anticipation. Mind you, I wasn't quite sure what 'Easy' was anticipating, possibly another feed.

My uncle patted my shoulder and said 'Now lad, I'm relying on you, this dog has to do his best. If I sell him, you know there'll be a wee cut for you in it.' I nodded weakly and looked at 'Easy' who sat there grinning from ear to ear. I might get a cut later on, but I didn't really expect it to involve money.

Anyway, there was no looking back now. I led 'Easy' to No. 5 trap and put him in after stroking his ears gently. He looked confused, as if he couldn't understand what was happening. The other dogs looked poised and ready for action.

I stepped back and considered making a run for it myself, but didn't. The bell rang, the electronic doors opened, the 'hare' shot off and so did the dogs. Yes, all of the dogs! I couldn't believe my eyes, 'Easy' was actually running and fast too. In fact, he went like the hammers of hell.

I could see Uncle Billy jumping up and down and cheering 'Easy' on. I started to yell too, he was a good five lengths in the lead! Yes, you've guessed it, Easy won by six lengths and at a price of 12/1! I don't know who was more surprised, Uncle Billy, me or 'Easy?'

The two buyers from Dublin were definitely impressed. They weren't going to be taken in too easily though, and decided to make sure it wasn't a fluke. Uncle Billy was to enter 'Easy' for another race next Saturday and if he performed as well that night, then they'd buy him.

Well, I was in a quare sweat and decided to confess all to my uncle. He couldn't believe it when I told him what 'Easy' had eaten that afternoon. He shook his head and said, 'Bobby my lad, we'll just have to try the same trick next Saturday and see what happens.'

So we did. Easy had a tremendous feed of cabbage and spuds and led the field home by six lengths again. This time we all had a wee bet on and he came in at 9/1. In fact, the story ended happily for everyone concerned as Uncle Billy decided not to sell 'Easy'.

He went on to make a lot of money out of him, as 'Easy' continued to do well and was soon travelling all over Ireland, running rings around the other dogs. I was his faithful companion and we stayed together until 'Easy' retired. By that time I had quite a bit stashed away and stayed in the business. Many other dogs, good and bad runners, passed through my hands, but never did one mean as much to me as 'Easy' did.

When he eventually died, I had him buried in my garden with a little plaque on the grave to honour him. It says *'Easy and Slow, a dog with a secret, and the best friend a man could have.'*

Now, this is a true story and I hope you've enjoyed it. I've been telling it to a wee girl who teaches in Jersey, you know one of those islands near France. She says she's going to write it down and enter it for some competition, but you can't always believe what a woman says, can you?

Alyson Meadowcroft is a retired teacher aged 62, living in Jersey since 1990. She is originally from Portaferry in Co. Down. Her story is based on a little tale told to her by a neighbour of her late mother, with a little bit of embellishment. Alyson has had a number of articles published in the Irish Times.

Rest in Peace, Tom Dooley

By Mary Weld,
Clane, Co. Kildare

*It is 1958 and the big treat after the Rosary every night is to be allowed
to tune in to Radio Luxembourg for an hour before going to bed. A song
by the Kingston Trio had a chorus that insidiously invaded our heads ...*

OUR FATHER ... Hail Mary ... Glory be... It was
always a relief to arrive at the fifth mystery of the
nightly Rosary, and for two reasons in particular.
Our nearly numbed knees could finally be prised from the
cold polished linoleum-floored parlour for another twenty
four hours and, even more important, Radio Luxembourg,
'The Station of the Stars', would shortly be turned on for an hour
before going to bed.

Tuning in was a procedure in itself, swirling the button along
the wave lengths was so funny. We would get snatched sounds
from a number of stations until we could finally hear the voice
of Horace Batchelor advertising his Infra-draw Method, which
was, believe it or not, a system he had worked out to win money
by predicting the results of football matches!

He would ask people to send him their name and address only
to Department One, Keynsham, spelt K-E-Y-N-S-H-A-M,
Bristol. We knew then we were tuned into Radio Luxembourg.

Oh what fun we would have singing along to the hits of Elvis,
Jerry Lee Lewis, Buddy Holly, Bobby Darin, Chuck Berry,

Pat Boone and Frankie Avalon, to name but a few. They sang about Peggy Sue, Johnny B. Goode and Billy, but the one that gripped our imaginations like no other was the ballad about Tom Dooley, sung in 1958 by the Kingston Trio.

This catchy tune was about a man who was convicted and hanged for the murder of his girlfriend in 1868. I still remember every word of it. The chorus went like this:

Hang down your head Tom Dooley,
Hang down your head and cry;
Hang down your head Tom Dooley,
Poor boy you're bound to die.

I don't know what it was about Tom Dooley, but we were definitely besotted by him. The ballad was all the time running through our heads. While walking home from school, or helping Mammy around the house, or even when lending a hand to Dad with the animals in the farmyard, we bellowed out the words of Tom Dooley.

If we heard a knock on the door we would smartly say 'It must be Tom Dooley', or if something could not be found we would blame Tom Dooley for taking it. We often asked Daddy if he met Tom Dooley when he was selling pigs at the fair, or even would remind Mammy to buy some extra broken biscuits in the shop for our special friend. It all became very silly really, and I don't know how our parents put up with us for so long. Of course it would only be a matter of time before it would all end badly.

One day my Dad was having a particularly difficult time as he tended to a sow giving birth to her piglets. She was very cross and restless, and he knew she would probably try to eat some of her piglets if they came anywhere near her mouth. He kept watch on one side of the farrowing crate and I kept watch on the other, and we pulled the piglets back if they were wandering into the danger zone of the sow's mouth.

The heat from the infrared lamps was ferocious, and the squeals from the sow were deafening. It was a big litter of piglets, and thankfully we were nearly there when, suddenly, we heard a loud roar from my brother as he ran from the house down into the yard.

'Daddy, Daddy come quickly,' he shouted, 'you are wanted on the phone'. It sounded extremely urgent. Wiping his hands with straw and uttering a string of expletives, Dad ran from the shed, and at the same time warned me to keep the piglets safe. I was nervous to be left on my own but it had to be done.

In a tormented voice Dad asked my brother 'Who wants me on the phone?' Accompanied with a big loud laugh my brother said 'Tom Dooley'!

The joke was finally over. It was over for us all. I can tell you Tom Dooley was FIRMLY put to rest in our house that day. His name was never mentioned again. Rest in Peace Tom Dooley, and thanks for the memories.

Mary Weld is married, and has three children and six grandchildren. She is retired, having worked for over forty years as an administrator in Maynooth University. She started writing in 2015 when she submitted her first story to Ireland's Own, *and this one is her second.*

Talking With My Father

By Richard Lysaght,
Walkinstown, Dublin

*Patrick visits his father regularly in hospital but there is
little meaningful conversation as his father has always been
a quiet, reserved man. With urging from his wife, Patrick
does attempt to talk to him, with surprising results …*

'HOW IS HE?' 'Having a nap at the moment,' the nurse grabbed my right arm and guided me down the hall, away from my father's room, and into the nurses' station.

'He is getting weaker, a lot weaker,' she said in a sombre voice, 'and he's eating less.'

'Is he in any pain?'

'None whatsoever, nor will he be, we make sure of that – I can assure you.'

'That's the main thing,' I said, nodding, and not knowing what else to say, said, 'did he eat much of his dinner?'

'Only the tiniest bit. Think he wore himself out chatting all morning to Father Moran, though I have to tell you,' her voice lightened, 'your father is some man when it comes to doing justice to jelly and ice cream; he polished off two bowls without any bother,' she said, smiling.

I would have smiled back but for being shocked by what she said, not that my father had polished off two bowls of jelly and ice cream; such a feat I witnessed my father perform every

16

evening from as far back as my memory reached. In fact, it used to amuse me, no end, when my school friends raved about getting jelly and ice-cream as a special treat, whereas for me it was an everyday occurrence, which is probably why I can't stand the stuff now.

Still jelly and ice-cream did make me popular amongst my friends, especially when they came to my house and my father offered them some, and being popular did lessen the gnawing sense of loneliness I often felt from not having a mother.

No, my shock came from hearing my father had spent the morning chatting. My father only ever said what needed to be said, never a word more, and now I was being told he had become garrulous, though I suppose I should have been buoyed by the news. After all, it would make the reason I had come here to St Martin's hospice at two in the afternoon instead of at eight in the evening, when I knew my father would be beginning to nod off, a lot easier.

I suppose, by now, you might be thinking my father and I were not close, and you would be right, and I suppose I may as well tell you the only reason I was visiting him at this time of day was in deference to my wife, Marise. She had been on to me (though 'badgered' would be nearer the mark) to have a meaningful talk, as she put it, with my father.

I left the nurses' station, thought to go home, let my father sleep and come back this evening at my usual time but the memory of last night's dinner conversation with Marise (same conversation we've been having every night for the past week) replayed in my mind.

'Patrick, you really need to have a talk with your father.'

'I do that every evening,' I said and added, 'by the way, this chicken casserole you made is delicious, no wonder I married you.' I speared a chunky piece of chicken with my fork, shoved it into my mouth, and made a loud mmm sound of approval.

'Don't be dodging the issue, Patrick'.

'I'm not dodging the issue'.

'Yes, you are.'

I looked across the table at Marise, her green eyes glowed with a look that was far from loving, and her chubby cheeks held a fiery hue which came perilously close to putting the bright red colour of her hair, which she kept tied back and tumbling past her shoulders, in the shade.

'You know practically nothing about your father after living with him for nearly thirty years, and if you don't take this chance to get to find out something about him now, it will soon be too late.'

'Not my fault,' I said. 'You know what he's like: he doesn't do talking, or have you forgotten?' I said, an edge of annoyance, which I didn't want to happen, slipping into my voice.

'Don't you be losing your cool with me, Patrick Kelly.'

'I'm most certainly not losing my cool; in fact, I'm as cool as a frozen cucumber.'

I forced a plastic smile onto my face.

'Yes, you are.'

This was getting ridiculous. Soon we would be having a full-blown argument over my father, and the last thing I wanted was for Marise to be upsetting herself, with fewer than six weeks to the birth of our first child. I needed to make her see sense, make her understand.

Marise came from a very loving and supporting family, which I knew made it difficult, if not impossible, for her to accept the kind of relationship I had, or didn't have, as the case may be, with my father. And to be fair, up to now, I had more or less given the subject of my father the shrug-of-the-shoulders and wave-of-the-hand treatment. I decided to try a different approach.

'Marise,' I said, in the softest voice I could manage, 'I really do appreciate and understand what you are saying. And, I have to admit, you are right; I should have a talk with my father, get to know something about him before he passes. And if he were a different kind of man, I can assure you that is exactly what I would do'.

I looked at Marise; her face was still on fire.

I sighed. 'Marise, think about what he worked at: fixing roofs and the higher up the roof was the better he liked it – church roofs he especially loved. He never socialized; never went to the pub, or had anyone calling to the house for a visit. He spent his free time pottering about in the shed down the garden, with a cigarette forever dangling from the side of his mouth.

'When he'd bring me out it was always to the Pictures, not that I'm complaining but you can't talk when you're at the Pictures. Even my mother he never spoke about, except at Mass on Sunday when he'd get me to light a candle for her'.

Now, I am in no way implying that he didn't miss her, he did. I would often catch him staring, for ages, at the photograph he kept of her on the sideboard, but he'd never say anything. Always keeps everything inside, that's my father, the way he is.

'I have no idea why he's that way. Maybe, he just never fitted in after moving here from England; maybe it's something to do with that, but, whatever it is, I feel that it is only right that I respect and accept him the way he is and, to be totally honest with you, I do. I hope you can understand that, Marise. Can you?'

I looked at Marise again, and felt a surge of delight and relief: the fire in her face was out; while in her eyes a gentle pensive-ness had taken up residence. I had finally gotten through to

19

her, made her understand. Indeed, I could feel the laurel wreath of victory being placed about my neck.

If I had just sat there and basked in the victory instead of opening my beak and saying, 'you know, Marise, if there was any way, and I mean any way at all, that I could get my father to open up, I would, but,' I let loose a long forlorn sigh, 'there just isn't.'

Marise nodded, her face suffused with sadness and then suddenly a beaming smile overtook the sadness as she said, 'I know a way.'

My father was sitting up in bed when I got back to his room. 'You're early.'

'Yes,' I said, clearing my throat. 'I came to have a chat with you about something but it's nothing that can't wait if you're feeling tired. The nurse said you had a busy morning.' I said, praying he would be too tired to talk.

'Sit down and tell me what you want to know.'

I looked at him, his blue eyes, the same colour as mine, were still clear and bright, his full head of white hair still thick and in no way receding, and his face, despite getting more gaunt, still held the high-colour of a life lived out of doors.

'Well,' I said, my heart pounding, 'Marise went for her final scan and she was talking to the doctor afterwards, and he was saying that it would be a good idea to know the medical history of the family, not that there is anything wrong, but just for future reference, that kinda thing.'

My father stared at the shelf at the bottom of the room where a statue of St Martin stood beside a lighted battery powered wax candle.

'I'm afraid I can't be of much help to you there.' He eased his head round and looked at me. 'You see, I was raised in an orphanage.'

'What?'

'Yes,' he sighed. 'I was one of those babies whose mother, for one reason or another, had to give them up. I was a few days old when my mother left me in a church. Father Kelly found me, wrapped in a blue blanket with a note from my mother saying that my name was Thomas and that she was sorry.'

I stared at my father, wanting to ask questions but afraid to interrupt him.

'Left the orphanage at sixteen and went working with a builder. I always liked working with my hands and being up on heights. I met your mother when I was in my thirties. I was fixing the roof of a house in Maidstone, in Kent. Your mother was nursing the elderly lady of the house.' My father shifted his gaze back to the shelf and became silent. For the next few minutes I listened to the wheezy sound of air going in and out of his lungs.

'Your mother and I hit it off straight away. She was an only child and, like me, had no one, both her parents were dead. We got married, moved here to Ireland and were very happy, doubly so when you were born. Your mother delighted in you, used to spend hours watching you sleep.'

My father became quiet again lost in memories and then after a heaving breath said, 'I suppose I should have told you all this before, but I am not someone who sees the point in dredging up the past. The past to me is like listening to an echo and believing someone's there.

'Only way I have ever learned to cope with what life dished out to me was always to keep moving on.' He paused and took a few more heaving breaths. 'Though, your mother's passing, when you were six years old, would have crushed me completely if I hadn't had you.' My father's eyes found mine.

'I suppose I should have spoken to you about your mother but,' his eyes returned to the statue and after a few moments said, 'I'm sorry, I haven't.'

'Absolutely no need to be sorry,' I said and then thinking about what Marise would tell me to do, I leaned over and, for the first time since I was a child, wrapped my arms around my father.

For almost a minute, I hugged a shop window dummy before I felt his right hand creep up my back followed by his left hand. Moments later, I felt the side of my face get wet and to save my father any embarrassment, I waited before pulling away. I also waited for my own tears to stop.

As I was leaving, I thought about buying Marise flowers and chocolates for convincing me to have this talk with my father and then when I reached the door, I remembered something else she said.

'By the way,' I said, turning to look at my father, 'Marise found out that she is having a boy. We are calling him Thomas Patrick.'

'Two good, strong names,' my father said, a smile lighting up his whole face. It was to be my last memory of him.

Richard Lysaght is retired after working for An Post for more than thirty years. He has three children and four grandchildren, who keep him physically active and mentally alert. He has been writing for as long as he can remember. He began with poetry and then turned to short stories, some of which have been published in Ireland and in England. He had a children's novel, Black Bag Mystery *published some years ago and is writing a novel for adults which should be finished by the end of 2017.*

Highland Laddie

By Annie May Harte,
Lifford, Co. Donegal

*A good dog was very important to a hill sheep farmer and when my
father's dog got too old a replacement was brought in from Scotland.
Laddie turned out to be very good which is why his disappearance
caused such consternation ...*

BACK IN THE 1950s, long before quads were heard
of, the sheep farmer depended on his sheep dog. My
father was a sheep farmer and his sheep were up on
the mountain. It was essential to own a good dog or two,
trained to go up the mountain range to round up the sheep
and bring them down to the low-lands. My father's dog had
gotten old and he was looking out for a good replacement.

Our dear friend, Father Tom McCabe, came home each year
from his parish in Scotland to spend time with his relatives in his
native Ballycarry. On one of his visits home, he asked Daddy if
he would like him to look out for a sheep dog for him. He told
my father that some of his parishioners were sheep farmers
and he would be on the look-out for a dog when he returned
to Scotland. My father was very pleased that the priest would
go to this trouble.

A few weeks after Father Tom had returned to his parish,
the phone call came to say that a Border Collie would be on
the Strabane train on the following Friday morning around

23

10 o'clock, having travelled over the previous evening on the Derry boat. My parents and brothers went to meet the train at Strabane to collect the much-awaited dog. They arrived back in Glenmornan with the dog in tow. My brothers carried the well-ventilated wooden box into the house.

Filled with excitement they opened the box and the dog emerged. He was a black and white coloured dog with a white ring around his neck and another on the tip of his tail. He was about six months old and his name was Laddie. We brought out a dish of food for him and he ate heartily. My brothers then took him for a walk along the Burn road. When they returned, it was as if Laddie had always lived at our house.

The next day, Daddy took him for his first run up the mountain. It wasn't long until they became inseparable, when you saw one, you saw the other. Daddy would be heard giving his commands: 'Come by Laddie; down dog, down; out wide; sit down, sit down.' Sometimes it was in a cross voice these commands were delivered. Daddy was always in control and obedience was a good sign in a dog.

Laddie proved to be very intelligent. He was soon able to go up the mountain on his own and bring the sheep down to Craignagapple where the sheep were dipped and clipped in early summer. When lambing season came in the spring, Daddy and Laddie were on the mountain all day long, watching for stray lambs and checking the sheep for foul foot.

Laddie settled in great on our farm and then one night the worst happened – the dog got lost. Daddy and Laddie were at Brockagh fair and as they were making their way home, a customs officer stopped them and began to search the car. As he opened the boot of the car, the dog jumped out and disappeared into the darkness. They called for ages but the dog didn't return that night.

My parents and brothers were distraught. Every night, my brothers and father would go back and call out the dog's name. Daddy would whistle but nothing happened. One night while they were searching, a neighbour called Timmy Doherty stopped in his car and asked them what was wrong. They explained to him about the dog being missing for over a week.

Timmy told them that a few days earlier he was talking to a night watchman who was working the late shift at the mill. The watchman had told him that a dog came to him every night and that he shared his food with him. My father asked him if they could go and see the night watchman and Timmy said they could. A short while later they were introduced to the man in question.

The watchman said the dog would come about eleven thirty. The time passed slowly but finally the dog came sauntering up the road. Daddy whistled and Laddie came running and jumped into his arms, licking his face and whining. They thanked the night watchman for minding the dog and headed home. Daddy and my brothers arrived back to our farm, delighted that the precious dog was found, well and bouncing with excitement.

Laddie lived to be a very old dog. It was a sad day that my father brought the faithful dog to the vet to have him put down.

Annie May Harte is a member of the Gateway Writers' Group in Lifford, Co. Donegal. This is her first time to feature in the Ireland's Own Anthology. *Her work has previously been published in the* Ireland's Own *weekly magazine.*

Coming Home

By Joe Duggan,
New Southgate, London

*He needed to speak to Callaghan and get it over with. He had
to tell him that he wouldn't be taking up the offer of moving
to Ireland, of working with him …*

THE TWO TWIGS floating lazily on the water were taken quickly by the current down between the mossy rocks towards the harbour, where Órla was waiting for them on the footbridge. 'Hurry Daddy!' she called excitedly to her dad, John, who had released the twigs and come running onto the bridge just in time to see them pass below.

'You win this time, Daddy,' Órla said leaning her head over the railing. 'Daddy, put them in again! Another race!' she said excitedly.

'Órla, we really must be going. Perhaps one more race but then we have to go. Mr Callaghan will be waiting for us in Rosslare.'

'But Daddy aren't we going to ride on the train?' Órla asked, pointing across the water to the red and yellow motorised train that took the children along the winding path beside the harbour; its ringing bell mingled with the holidaying children's voices, and the cries of seagulls gliding low on the late summer breeze.

'I'm afraid we must be going,' said John. His mind was anxious; they just had to get on to Rosslare because he'd made up his mind and he had to act on it – whatever had possessed him to take the detour from the main road? He should have known it would be impossible to hurry Órla from the seaside.

Perhaps he should have come over from England on his own in the first place, he mused. It wasn't so much they were late, but he needed to speak to Callaghan and get it over with. He had to tell him that he wouldn't be taking up the offer of moving to Ireland, of working with him, and he wanted to tell him face to face. Callaghan deserved that.

But it was on the Dublin-Wexford road, an hour out from Dublin Port, that he'd seen the sign for the harbour, the little seaside town of his childhood summer holidays, a memory from his past that seemed to whisper to him, to turn off the road, see again the little town. He hadn't been here for almost forty years.

Órla had slipped her little hand into his on the bridge and was now leading him along the path beside the harbour towards the train, her smile looking up at him meant she was going to get her way. And with the light off the water on her face, the tussle of her hair in the breeze, she was reminding John so much of his own mother, and continuing along he felt his urgency and anxiety to get on the road ease a little.

'Ok, Órla,' he said resignedly. 'One ride on the train, but then we have to go.'

They waited in the queue for the train beside the harbour, with its rocking masts and swooping gulls. How little the town had changed since he was a boy – the footbridge, the harbour, just as John remembered it; over to the left, the grassy hill path, the way up to the caravan parks. Had there been a coffee shop half way up? A cinema by the arcade? And as he was remembering, behind them not far off, still the sound of the sea, rolling pebbles back and forth across the beach.

The boat-train from Manchester Victoria snaked its way out of the station it was so long, and then wound its way around the North-Wales coast, and John and his brother, Pax, with their heads out the window all the way. Then the queue up to the Holyhead boat – the Hibernia, or perhaps the Cambria. Like refugees they were with their bags and cases tied with string; John with his brothers and sister – she holding her doll – and their mother.

Hours later, he'd run from the decks to tell her that he could see her home, just a grey outline at first in the distance. 'Oh can you, John?' she'd say. 'Can you see it?' Then Ireland appeared in colour out of the sea – the twin sisters of Dublin port with their flashing beacons; Sugarloaf Mountain, Dalkey Island, and then past the little lighthouse on Dun Laoghaire pier.

He would look up at his mother's face just then to see her look of sublime happiness because she was home, but it was a happiness touched always by a melancholy that she could never conceal.

He sat beside Órla in the little carriage, in her red coat, hair blowing gently against her happy face. She pointed excitedly out at the seagulls, and at the small boats bobbing on the water. The bell rang as the little train continued up beside the harbour towards the RNLI station, above which the last of the summer sun shone like a golden coin in the sky.

There was barely a brass farthing when they landed at Dun Laoghaire. They'd be met by their uncle Paddy from the boat, and spend a few days in Dublin before travelling down with a few of the cousins to Wexford. How seven or sometimes eight of them managed to squeeze into Paddy's little car was a wonder.

They would spend their days on the beach, or among the dunes. In the late afternoon they'd be fishing by the harbour, trying to catch a mullet for dinner. Uncle Paddy would make them up a rod on their first day, with a cork for a float, and a steel nut for a weight to throw out. A mullet would have made a nice change from the soup. Sometimes they would run out of the bottled gas at night, and that would be the end of the money until a registered letter arrived from their dad back in Manchester to keep them going. John still remembered the anticipation of a registered letter – there might be a cup of coffee the next day in that café on the hill, or perhaps a bag of chips in the evening. Then back in the caravan John's mother would tell the stories of Irish folklore – The Children of Lir and Tuatha De Danaan; the Dagda; the Banshee – before settling them all to bed. They all loved her stories in the darkness waiting for sleep. Their happiness had been the simplicity of their day, and the soft fading melody of a mother's Irish lullaby.

Well it was all right for Callaghan, he could turn his hand to anything. And he did. He could build a house from top to bottom if he had a mind. He had his own plant nurseries just outside Enniscorthy. If there was an arrangement of pretty flowers in a posh Dublin shop, Callaghan had put them there. He did a roaring trade at Christmas and Easter, and again near Valentine's. He owned the vans that made the deliveries. In the summer, he sold Wexford strawberries from Kerry as far up as Sligo. 'Come over,' he had said to John in Manchester, 'and together we can work a little magic.' And it was decent of Callaghan to ask. He wanted no investment in return – he had known John's father. But what if he got sick? What if he hurt his hand? How would they survive?

All this was on John's mind as they made their way from the train, and he was fully aware that Órla was now guiding him by the hand in the direction of the ice creams on the other side of the bridge. But he did not protest. What was the harm?

He would let Órla enjoy her afternoon, they would take their time. Perhaps he would call Callaghan. They could make their way back to Dublin, catch the early ferry in the morning.

He believed he did not have the talents to survive here. He did not have the skills to get by, he couldn't turn his hand to anything like Callaghan could, despite his friend's faith in him. Yet at the same time, John thought as they made their way back across the bridge now with their ice creams, if they were going to make the move this was the time to do it.

And heaven knows it had been tough enough back in England. He had been made redundant from his job two years before, and he now had two jobs to make up the week, neither of which he enjoyed much, but perhaps things would change for the better if he could stick it out. It wouldn't be fair on Órla to chance things over here; it would be too risky. Surely it would be too risky?

Órla broke off a piece of her cone and threw it awkwardly for a seagull that caught it expertly as it swooped out across the water.

'Daddy, can we catch a fish?' she asked. Mullet manoeuvred continuously to conceal themselves in the shadows under boats that drifted and swayed about their moorings.

'Those things are very difficult to catch, Órla. When Daddy was a boy, he tried to catch them.'

'Did you ever catch one, Daddy?'

'No, darling ...' he said, but then that whispered memory, silently telling him that there was that one time ... he had almost forgotten ... just that one time when he was a boy.

They had come down from the caravan park in the early evening. The boys had adjusted the weights and the float, and on their way down had fine-tuned the doughy bread for bait with their fingers; the girls ambled behind uninterested, with his sister, Molly, who had been feeding her dolly with the doughy bread.

The harbour teemed with mullet; they shifted themselves under boats as the last of the evening's sun glistened on the water. But it wasn't long before their lack of interest at being caught was having its effect, and the cousins began to wander. The girls ambled by the pier. Pax was over by the bridge being smart with a couple of the Dublin lads. Molly stayed; she was tugging at John's elbow to leave as he cast out for the last time, the last of the doughy bread. She tugged again. 'Molly,' he said impatiently to her. There was another tug but this time from the water. John had caught his fish.

It was Molly's excited jumping that brought the cousins running, Pax was ahead of them with the Dublin lads, shouting to John to keep a hold of it. Its strength was fierce, but John was determined to reel it in. About a foot from the edge he lifted its head from the water, but in an effort to break free it gave an almighty swish of its tail and leaping out landed straight into the waiting arms of John. He couldn't believe his luck. The mullet was still.

'It's massive,' said Pax, leaning on John's shoulder. They all gathered round to look, as the last rays of the evening sun sparkled on the water, and on the scales of the mullet in John's arms, giving the fish a wondrous golden glow, illuminating the faces of the children gathered round.

'Sure, it's the Salmon of Knowledge!' one of the Dublin lads shouted sarcastically, and in that instant John lifted his arms, releasing the great fish, which, with a swish of its tail, dived gracefully back into its harbour home.

The walk back up to the caravan was an eternity for him – Pax was niggling and pushing him all the way; even Molly, mimicking the Irish cousins, had called him 'such a big eejit,' as she walked along with her dolly. But back in the caravan his mother was laughing.

She took a frying pan and tapped John on the head with it saying, 'And here was me waiting for my lovely fish and my frying pan all eager … and what's that, Pax?' she asked. 'The Salmon of Knowledge? Well why not indeed, why shouldn't he be down from County Meath on his holidays? And to think, John,' she said, 'to think by touching him you've gained such wisdom …'

The warm evening breeze came off the sea, as John and Órla walked barefoot in the shallow surf. There was no rush now. John knew that. They could take their time. Órla looked up at him with her happy face. 'Daddy,' she asked, 'can we come here again?'

'All the time, Órla. Would you like that?'

'Yes, Daddy.' She was so like her granny in many ways. And in so many ways they would all be coming home.

This is the first time that Joe Duggan has had anything published, though he has always wanted to write. He is 54 and is originally from Manchester. He moved to London about 15 years ago. Both parents were born in Ireland, and he is one of four siblings, all of whom still live there. His parents died not too long ago. Ellen and Joe have a daughter, Órla (he couldn't resist using her name in the story!) and he works as a Welfare Officer in schools across Barnet in North London.

A Terrible Lie

By Paul McLaughlin,
Marmount Gardens, Belfast

Billy Webster ran a bustling butchery business in Belfast but he craved acceptance in more 'elite' circles and joining the Masons gave him a route-one entrance to the golf club, the tie and all the right connections. Life could not be better …

GETTING MEMBERSHIP of the Royal Lodge Golf Club had proved an impossibility for Billy Webster until he'd become a Freemason. Like it or not, and his late father, once a well-known Belfast trade unionist, would have disapproved thoroughly. Joining the Masons gave Billy a route-one entrance to the club, the tie and all the right connections.

Billy, with a bustling butchery business on the far side of thriving, once tied to the ceremonial apron strings, was guaranteed good contacts, even better business and an occasional game of golf into the bargain.

He had a lot to be thankful for and he knew it. The free meat parcels for his sponsoring member, Melvyn Armstrong, were a small price to pay in the scheme of things and Billy, at 32, with a quiet wee wife, two kiddies and a newly-built detached house, looked forward to getting all he could from the 'Lodge', as it was known locally.

Not that he looked like a sportsman of any description, albeit a golfer. William, as his mother still insisted on calling him, had been the boy who could not get a game of football, despite owning the ball. His roundness of face was complemented by a body that was built for comfort rather than speed.

The thinning mousey-coloured hair, thick spectacles and Zapata moustache only confirmed the undeniable fact that Billy's place in life was behind the shop counter at 'Webster's, The Family Butcher'. He had been born to wear the brown shop coat, his right ear the perfect pencil holder, but he had dreams and, with his entry to the 'Lodge', they had started to come true.

'Welcome aboard, Bill,' said the Club President, Richard McIntyre, known to all as 'Spotted Dick' on account of the polka dotted bow ties he wore beneath his Pringle sweaters, after the vote at the Thursday session of the committee. "Play up and play the game" is the motto and you're just the kind of chap to do us proud. This is one decision you won't regret'.

Billy, blushing to his sparse roots with a mixture of pride and embarrassment, managed to say, 'I only regret things that I didn't do, Richard' and left it at that. He didn't trust himself not to make an eejit of himself with some sort of fawning accept-ance speech. But, oh my, it was just as he had imagined it would be – terribly middle-class, everyone pronouncing their 'ings' and business being done at a phenomenal rate, but with discretion of course. Discretion was everything in a secret society.

The Masonic had been a step up for the wee boy from the terraced house in Greenmount Street and he'd loved all that special handshake kind of stuff, especially the dressing-up paraphernalia, but the nod from the 'Lodge' confirmed his arrival on the social scene.

His wife, Marjie, seemed overawed by the news, perhaps a little less enthusiastic than he would've hoped, but he knew that her new frock for the Saturday evening supper dance hung expectantly in the wardrobe. 'M' and 'B', as they used to call one another in the early days of their twelve-year marriage, were now on the 'A' list, which was just as it should be.

'Not bad, Mammy,' said Billy on his weekend duty visit to the Webster family home. 'I'm in with the elite of the city now, a full blown member of the 'Lodge' and I already have Marjie's name down for the women's charity committee as a wee surprise. She'll love it, I know.'

Mrs Webster, a widow since her husband Harold had been machine-gunned on a positively non-blue flag beach outside Dunkirk in 1940, frowned a fan of lines across a large fore-head and surveyed her only child.

'Well, William, you're the man your grandfather would have been proud to call son. The Websters were building boats in this town since the shipyard opened, but you're the first to break out of the kitchen house. You're a man of business, who has no time for the pub or the bookies and you'll do well for yourself. I'm so proud of you.'

As it happened, Billy was even more proud of himself as he stood on the half moon rug in front of a hissing coal fire, watching himself in the tiny over-mantle mirror, his chest puffing out ever so slightly like a budgie about to ring a bell. He wasn't sure how shipbuilding fitted in with filleting, but he let it go.

'I've written to your Auntie Madge with the good news, William', said mother, 'and you're the talk of Co Tyrone. Why, her whole family are as jealous as the jilted.'

Billy's chest expanded like a Charles Atlas advert with her every word and his kiss on her blue-waved hair was moist and sincere.

'I'm off to play golf this afternoon, Mammy, so I can't be hanging around. There's talk of another shop becoming available on the Albertbridge Road pretty soon, but I'll have to wait 'til I get the word from a brother Mason at the estate agents. I'll ring you later as always. Bye, bye pet.'

Billy closed the vestibule door with a wave and left his mother to her antimacassars and Earl Grey tea.

'God, what a great wee woman,' he thought as he steered the Morris Oxford into the Beersbridge Road. 'Left alone to rear a son and her only a slip of a girl herself. She's done us both proud.'

'Always new clothes for a set time, the first telephone in the street, even the sunburned Summer holidays in Portrush each year while the youngsters at home lined the street like milk bottles. Aye, and on her own, Mammy did the lot on her own. A great wee woman.'

Billy drove out toward the suburbs with a warm feeling under his hounds-tooth jacket, happy in the knowledge that he was loved and that Jackie McKenna, his charge-hand, was looking after business. Jackie was a born bachelor and a born-again Christian, interviewed for the job by his mother nearly five years before and recommended by Pastor McIlwaine from their church as an honest man in a land of rogues and RCs.

Well into his fifties, practically a friend of the family, dapper Jackie often 'babysat' for Mammy on weekday evenings when Billy put either the family or the Masonic first. Jackie also looked after the family garden in Bloomfield and did most of the DIY around the home. Marjie and the kids adored him. They were always singing his praises, especially Marjie. She really thought the world of him, and she a good Christian woman herself.

Billy thought to himself, taking a precariously sharp left turn onto the Woodstock Road, 'We're lucky to have old Jack. He's a real brick and I'll see him right with a wee increase in his pay packet'. Minutes later as he strode across the car park to the clubhouse, Billy spoke out loud to no-one in particular, 'No better man than Jackie. He deserves at least a small rise after all these years.'

Billy headed off for a four-ball with a florid-faced chap from the abattoir, whose ample stomach led the way, and two new friends from the Ministry of Agriculture with a beatific look on his reddening face.

Business was brisk at Webster's that Saturday afternoon. Jackie had donned the brown manager's coat and the owner's air of authority, while under-hand Eric Cardwell and teenage apprentice Wesley McFadden cut, sliced, wrapped and parcelled Sunday dinners for suburban East Belfast.

The two younger men laughed and chatted over ribs and sausages like two gastric surgeons at the City Hospital, but Jackie said nothing and smiled only for paying customers. His earnest evangelical face ensuring his distance from the other staff and the degree of respect guaranteed. The distance suited Jackie, the respect was an added bonus to a meagre wage from a mean employer.

Billy scored 37, won the Stableford competition that afternoon and bought drinks all round at the 19th with a light heart and a heavy wallet.

'Marjie can drive home tonight for a change,' he thought, 'Or we'll leave the car until tomorrow. There's a bit of celebratin' to do and he dropped the 'ing' in his head without a worry.

Three or four drinks later, Billy's face was as red as a wee boy caught carrying on in chapel, his voice raised like a riveter and his laughter raucous across the bar. But everyone, even 'Spotted Dick', whose own uncle had held a particularly well-gerrymandered seat in the Stormont parliament for more than 30 years, was knocking them back.

The assembled vowels got broader and flatter as the booze hit the mark and the inner city came out treacherously in the inner man. Everyone agreed, loudly, that Billy Webster, 'Specky Billy' from Greenmount Street, who had never hit a ball in anger, had played the best seventeen holes of his life.

'Lord above,' said Billy to his excited companions, each one replaying the best and worst of a spoiled afternoon's walk; 'I forgot to phone me Ma. I always ring her at teatime to make sure she's okay.' And with that he swagger-staggered off to the mock, red telephone kiosk that stood like a sentry box against the wall of the members' lounge.

Mammy's voice answered, confused and scratchy like an old record and just as repetitive. 'I don't know what's happening, William. I just don't know what's happening. Marjie's left a letter for you and headed off in the car. I just don't know what's happening.'

'A what?' said Billy; 'Read it out, woman. It must be important.'

He waited for a long two minutes, beating the pips on the coinbox with another sixpence inserted just in time as the old woman searched for her reading glasses. His breath came in snorts, his alcohol-fuelled pulse pumping in his ear and his patience fraying by the second.

'For heaven's sake woman, read the cursed thing,' he shouted down the line, but Mrs Webster was in the parlour, oblivious to his profanity.

Eventually she read: 'It says, no she says, "Jackie and I have taken the kids and the money the taxman knew nothing about and we are heading to Scotland to start a new life. I am sick to death of the spoilt wee boy with the big …"'

'What Ma? Is that you Ma? What the heck's goin' on?'

Billy, the drink dying in him, with two agile fingers waved away a fellow clubman who had banged on the door to use the 'phone.

"The spoilt wee boy with the big ideas," she says Mammy continued: "It's over and thank God. I hope your Masonic and your 'Lodge' put a smile on your fat, red face. Your other woman can keep you. God love her, she deserves you. Good-bye and good riddance, Marjie".' The old woman's voice tailed off in a confused snuffle of linen and sobs.

'Other woman, William' she screeched, 'What other woman? You can't have another woman. People in our church don't have other women. What does it mean, William? We'll be the talk of the congregation. Tell me it's not true, Billy.'

'No Mammy. That's one terrible lie, I tell you. One terrible lie.'

As Billy's words echoed loud and clear from the little kiosk, his playing partner, Archie Walls, reported back to the boys at the bar that the 'Bold Bill' was already 'making excuses to his mammy' for his disaster on the eighteenth hole.

Paul McLaughlin, married with one son, is a former journalist with BT public relations. Semi-retired, he now works part-time for the Northern Ireland Mixed Marriage Association and has written two books about mixed marriage in Ireland. He had his first story published in Ireland's Own *nine years ago and has featured regularly in the* Ireland's Own Anthologies.

'Are You Rightly John Smith?'

By Jim Gammons,
Virginia, Co. Cavan

*Recalling a man who acted as 'The people's solicitor' in West
Cavan and was an invaluable guide to a housing inspector
travelling the by-roads and trying to unravel the mysteries of
nick names by which many people were known.*

MANY YEARS AGO I was a Housing Inspector administering a scheme of minor subsidies called 'Housing Grants'. In the 1950s, my territory was Leitrim with an odd foray into West Cavan. West Cavan, above all else, meant John Smith from Bawnboy. Most country people at the time preferred the spade to the pen and left the filling up of forms to the local wise man, in this case, John Smith 'the people's solicitor'.

My colleagues and I started our visits in West Cavan by calling on John Smith. The first business was 'the tea', as John's wife Janey automatically reached for the tea pot as soon as anyone came in the door. To quote Father McKiernan at her funeral, 'She made as many cups of tea as there are stars in the sky'. Everyone that came in to céilí or have a form filled up got the tea. It was a ritual.

John welcomed being asked to come out on calls as it was a break from the farm work and it was the sort of social day he loved. Everyone gained, as often my day was burdened with calls to random houses to find out where does 'so and so' live. John knew everyone from Belturbet to Blacklion, so the time that would have been wasted on enquiries was spent on chatting and tea drinking.

Talking about enquiring, I spent a whole morning many years ago enquiring for an Owen McGovern of Derrynanta, Glangevlin. I stopped a man almost at random and asked for 'Owen McGovern of Derrynanta'. This was over fifty years ago and there were lots of people and lots of houses around then. He said, 'There's 13 Owen McGoverns in Derrynanta. You'll have to tell me more about him'.

I said, 'The only other thing I know about him is that he has a bad house'. He said, 'That narrows it down to 9'.

Coming up to lunch time and a dozen enquiries later I found I was looking for 'Ownie Einy Atty' and his sister 'Annie Einy Atty'. Everyone has a nick name involving father's and grandfather's names and without that knowledge you were lost. Ownie's father was also Owen, spelt Eoin and pronounced Ein, as in the German for 'one' and his grandfather was Matty, pronounced 'Atty'.

Another time I was looking for a James McGovern and kept failing because I didn't know his nick name. I came across a postman leaning on his bicycle and talking to another man. I said to myself, 'postmen know everyone, I'm in business'.

When I put the question to the postman he said, 'Would it be this man here?'

I said, 'It could be, but I have no way of knowing'. Several different expressions crossed the postman's face. So he looked at his companion as much as to say, 'You sort it out'.

The companion said 'Would it be about a grant for a house?' I said, 'Yes'. I had found my man. It was in fact, Jimmy

Hun I was looking for and the postman's friend was Hun. The postman didn't want to say 'Is it Jimmy Hun you're looking for?' in case the nickname might give offence.

I did my business and went away thinking Jimmy's father was probably in the British Army in the first World War and came home full of vivid stories about killing 'Huns'. The real explanation was completely different and I heard it from a lady called Eithne McGovern, a native of Glan.

'I knew Jimmy Hun' she said. 'His grandparents spoke Irish. His mother spoke a mixture of Irish and English and objected to old people calling her son 'A mhic' which sounds like 'a vick'. She called him 'A son', the seíbhú turning the 's' into a h'.

John Smith never asked 'How are you?' He said, like all the old people in West Cavan, 'Are you rightly?' I remember calling into a farmyard in deep West Cavan many years ago with John Smith in the car with me. When we pulled up in the yard a middle aged woman was feeding calves at a gate from two buckets. She was wearing a sacking apron but when she heard the car behind her she threw it off and turned towards the car to greet her visitors.

She looked first at the driver (me). Her incipient smile disappeared when she saw it was a stranger. When she looked at the other side of the car the sun came out again. 'Are you rightly, John Smith?' rang out. The response was 'Are you winnin' Mary Kate?' The Russian communists dreamt of building a community like that, but it can't be built. It has to grow out of the soil.

Jim Gammons was born in Rathkenny, Co. Meath in 1930. He qualified as a Civil Engineer and joined the Department of Local Government as a Housing Inspector in 1953. He covered football for the Meath Chronicle and reported the *Meath football tour of Australia for the* Irish Times *in 1968. He married Lillian in 1969 and moved to Virginia, Co. Cavan. In 1995 he edited* Virginia Golf Club – The first 50 years *and also produced two books,* Virginia Then and Now *and* Virginia 400. *He also edited* Meath of the Pastures, *a collection of his father's prose and poetry. He retired as Senior Inspector for the six northern counties in 1995 and writes now mostly for* Ireland's Own.

Just the Ticket

By Kevin Martin,
Westport, Co. Mayo

Peter wants to go to his first All-Ireland final with his dad to support his county team but, as always, tickets are scarce. The match ends in a draw, which gives everyone a second chance, and help comes from an unexpected source ...

'DADDY, YOU MUST know someone who could get us tickets for the final. Paul has got one and he never goes to any of the matches. You have to know somebody'.

My son Peter rarely asks for anything. I had entered three draws: one at Supervalu, one on a card from the GAA club and another to raise funds for a new school extension in the next parish and, as usual, I had no luck with any of them. I even rang Anna's cousin, Father Tom in Cavan – and he is not an easy man to talk to – and he couldn't help. If priests can't get their hands on these things there isn't much hope for the likes of me.

'Who has tickets from your class anyway?'

'Everyone has,' said Peter.

'Who is everyone?'

'Well Jimmy and Philip and Paul like I said ...'

'Jimmy's father is President of the GAA club and Philip's mother is a doctor, so of course they have tickets. Unfortunately that's the way things work in this country, Peter. No one knows exactly what Paul's father does but he always seems to have a new car or van. The world works in mysterious ways and they are a complete mystery to me. I don't even have a job.'

Peter didn't look me in the eye. 'I know that. It's just that I really think they have a chance this year. Now that they have a good full back line I think they can do it.'

I couldn't help smiling. He was hearing this talk among the coaches and the lads at the club. Despite his best intentions Peter had never mastered the subtleties of Gaelic football. He just didn't have it in him the way I had or Tim, my brother, had. It was an awful pity Tim never stuck at it but then there were no jobs around and he ended up in Coventry and, of course, it was the usual story with the drink after that. It was the knees with me.

'Well I hope you're right. They got caught out the last time under the high ball. It was over before it started,' I said.

'You're right there Dad,' said Peter.

That was the Monday evening before he went down to the pitch for training with the under-14 lads. The week before the game was long. The weather was bad and no one wanted hedges or lawns cut and you couldn't get outside to do any painting. I didn't even have the price of a few pints to go over and watch the match in the pub on the Sunday, so myself and Peter sweated it out in the sitting room. We hardly spoke the whole time.

'Can you believe that Dad? When was the last time that there was a draw in a football final?'

I could remember the game but didn't want to get into it. It was the year Tim said he had got tickets in Coventry and asked me to come up to Dublin and meet him to go to the match. He told me afterwards he fell and couldn't travel but I heard he didn't get past his local pub.

'At least they didn't get caught out in the full back line. That new corner back is a great lad. I'd say he was first to every ball in the match,' he said.

'You're right son. They've tightened up a lot. I know their record in replays isn't great but they could do it the next day'.

The replay was announced for October 1, the day Peter would turn 12. I knew he wouldn't even mention a ticket this time. There wasn't a lot of talk around the town about the match. If you lose one replay you're afraid of them.

I got three days work the week before the replay, power-hosing the paths around old Mrs Walsh's place, not the easiest of work, but the money was handy. It was nearly seven o' clock on Friday before I finished it. When I got back down to our own place there was an English-registered car in the front yard. You'd see plenty of them during the summer around the place but not this time of the year. I was fairly worried going into the house. Anna opened the door just before I got to it.

'We have a visitor and you're never going to guess who it is.' She was flushed.

'It's not bad news is it?' I asked.

Before she could answer Tim poked his head around the sitting room door.

'How's the baby brother then?'

He looked well. The yellow tinge was gone from his skin and his grey eyes glistened.

'What are you doing here? Where did you get the fancy wheels from?' I asked.

'That's a nice way to say hello. I'm home for the match. The car is rented.'

'It's a long time since you showed any interest in going to see a match. What's the story?'

'I've always been interested in the matches. I'd have come more often if I had the money and the health but there have been a few rough times over the last few years,' he said.

'So what has changed this year that brings us the pleasure of your company?'

'Well, I have a job for a start and I gave up the drink last Christmas. That was a big help'.

'How do you propose to get your hands on tickets? They're like gold dust around here. Unless you're in with the right crowd you haven't a chance of getting one.'

'I've never had much luck in my life and I know I created a lot of my own misfortune but you could say I got a lucky break'.

He produced two Hogan Stand tickets from the inside pocket of his corduroy jacket. It wasn't the right length in the arms but I couldn't remember him ever wearing one before.

'I was doing a painting job out in Leeds for an old woman, a lovely old lady called Margaret Joyce. Her father was from over on the island and we had great crack during the few days I was out with her.'

'Did she pay you well?' I asked.

'Well she didn't have much to her name, I'd say. The husband had died years ago but apparently he was very involved in the GAA over there. A Westmeath man, I think. But anyway she was paying me on the Friday evening and she asked me if I would have any use for these two boyos here.'

He held the tickets up.

'The old lad had been sent them for his involvement over the years. It was the 25th anniversary of the founding of the club. They didn't even know he was dead. So you better get yourself ready to go to the big smoke.'

I knew I could not go without Peter.

'If anyone deserves a bit of luck it's you Tim,' I said.

'So come on then. Start getting ready. Up first thing in the morning and make a weekend of it. Have a look around some of the old haunts. You'd never know who you might bump into.'

I was tired and told him I had to go to bed. I couldn't sleep. At around two I heard a creak coming from the kitchen which I knew to be the door of the fridge. I got up to check and could see Tim at the kettle making tea.

'Tim I need to talk to you. It's about the match tomorrow.'

'You're not getting cold feet or anything? I know they've lost a few since the last time but that's no reason to stay at home. Go on and get some sleep and you'll be rearing to go in the morning.'

'I couldn't go and leave Peter at home. He loves the game a lot more than I do and it just wouldn't be fair to him. He'd never understand.'

'I was thinking I didn't explain myself properly. The tickets are for Peter and you. I'm not going to it. Sure how many times have I let you down in the past? Not alone did drink nearly kill me, it ruined every bloody relationship I ever had. You know, my life changed after that thing about the tickets a few years ago. I was ashamed of myself.'

'I got awful low after that. I went in on myself a bit to be honest. You never held it against me. You still wrote. You still sent me a Christmas card. For a couple of years it was the only one I got and I'm not ashamed to say, it had to be brought to me in a park because I wasn't living in any house for a while but I had a few old mates who looked out for me.'

I could feel my chin quivering. I'm not a man given to crying normally but it was hard to keep it in.

'You were and are a great brother to me, a true brother. Now, that's all I can say before I make a fool of myself. Take these and get a bit of sleep.'

I thanked him but I don't know if I did it right. And I still don't.

'You'll be coming up with us?'

'No. I'm staying in the hotel in town for a few nights. I want to try and meet a few of the old crowd, clean up the grave and a few other things. I'll see ye when ye get back with the cup.'

They say it was one of the greatest All-Irelands ever played. The action went from end to end. You could hardly get your breath. I never saw Peter so excited about anything. He said afterwards that it was the best day of his life. It was hard to believe it went down to the last kick of the ball for a second time and for once we came out on the right side.

The Sam Maguire came to the town for the first time ever on the Monday night. We only just got down in time from Dublin. Maybe Tim knew, because he had the best view of us all, looking out a window of the hotel. After the speeches and the presentations it was nearly one o' clock before I got talking to him. His eyes were watery.

'I didn't watch it at all. I'm gone too nervous. It destroys me. I spent the morning up at the graveyard. I did a bit of tidying up on the grave and put in a few plants and that but I saw it on The Sunday Game. Unbelievable.'

Peter was beside me so I think I mentioned something about pride in the county and the family. I can't quite remember because I had a good few pints by then and I'm not used to drinking.

'Well I hope you are because you have a great young son there and like I said, you've been a great brother to me. I'm off to England in the morning so I'm going to head for the bed now. Thank God I lived to see this day. Good luck. I'll see ye soon please God. Ye will have to come over. We might go to a soccer game. What do you think Peter?'

'I'd love that Uncle Tim.'

Kevin Martin is 48, married to Maria with two children, Caitlin (13) and Joey (11). He worked as a lecturer in Personal Development at the Institute of Technology in Blanchardstown, Dublin, but took early retirement to bring up the children. His first book, Have Ye No Homes To Go To? The History of the Irish Pub, *was published by The Collin's Press (Cork).*

The Lad who Played with Meccano

By Kevin McDermott,
Crossabeg, Co. Wexford

He went to a classmate's house to see his Meccano set but he didn't receive much of a reception from his mother because she considered him from 'the wrong part of town'. After school their paths diverged until he saw him in London years later ...

HE WAS WHAT my mother would call 'a big lump of a lad' and he sat in the seat in front of me in our school classroom. I didn't really have much to do with him until the day I heard him telling a friend about the lovely Meccano set he had received for Christmas. I have to admit I felt very envious and I asked him all about it. I was pleasantly surprised when he invited me to call to his house that evening to have a look at it.

He lived in a semi-detached house on the outskirts of the town, and I was full of anticipation when I arrived on his doorstep and rang the bell. He opened the door and invited me in to the lounge where the Meccano set was spread out on a table. I was not disappointed, it was everything I had imagined and more. I watched fascinated as he worked feverishly on a fire engine he was trying to build from the many small parts that came with the set.

51

I was so engrossed that I didn't notice his mother had entered the lounge. 'Who is he and where is he from?' she enquired in a rather brusque manner. 'He's in my class at school', he replied, 'and he wanted to see my Meccano set.' However, when she found out that I came from the council houses on the opposite side of town, she reacted angrily and admonished her son.

'How often have I told you to keep away from that kind', she said, and addressing me, she told me, in no uncertain terms, that she didn't want to see me around here again. I was only eleven years old but I felt it wouldn't be fair to relate the incident to my mother. I knew her feelings would be just as hurt as mine.

When eventually our schooldays ended, he and I went our separate ways, he to a college and me to the local technical school. Although I saw him on many occasions in our teens we never interacted socially. Eventually, due to unemployment I was forced to leave Ireland and join the thousands of my fellow countrymen and women who were leaving to seek their fortune on foreign shores. In the 1950s I boarded the Princess Maud for Holyhead and England.

The years went by and in the mid 1960s I was in my seventh year as a fire-fighter with the London Fire Brigade. It was a Saturday afternoon and I was now a junior officer on duty at a busy fire station in a market area of East London. I was working on some fire reports in the station office when I noticed a group of firemen gathered around an upstairs window. They were watching an incident unfolding in the street below.

They told me jokingly that one of my countrymen was having a go at the police, so I joined them at the window. Sure enough, in the middle of the busy road, stood a scruffy looking man who was stripped to the waist. He looked to be very drunk and was shouting abuse in a broad Irish accent at the two constables who were standing on the pavement. The constables left him to it and concentrated on controlling the traffic while they awaited the arrival of the police van.

When the vehicle arrived it had another couple of policemen aboard and all four closed in on the noisy Irishman in the middle of the road. After some resistance and more shouting they managed to push him into the back of the van they had parked on the forecourt of the fire station. Just before the doors closed he looked up at us watching from the window.

It was only then I saw his face clearly and I froze. It was him. The same lad that sat in front of me at school, and whose mother felt I was not good enough for him to play with. It was about ten years since I had last seen him but I had no doubt, it was him alright. When the van was loaded and the rear doors secured, it drove off to the local police station and our paths never crossed again. Some years later I heard he had died in London.

In the fire station I made my way to the engine room and stood looking at the gleaming red fire engine parked there ready for action. A tear trickled down my cheek as I thought of watching 'the big lump of a lad' with his Meccano set trying to build a fire engine all those years ago. May he rest in peace.

Kevin McDermott was born in Cavan town; he emigrated to England in 1955 but he returned to live in Crossabeg in 1990 with his wife Noreen. They have two sons, James and Ronan. He spent 25 years as a London firefighter. He is an accomplished musician, and enjoys acting and performing comedy recitations. In 2004 he published his autobiography The Time of the Corncrake. *He has recorded a CD of recitations* 'Many Miles of Potholed Road' *which included three of his own compositions, and to celebrate his 80th birthday in 2016 he recorded a CD of some of his favourite accordion music called* 'Musical Gems from a Button Box'.

Flamingo

By Martin Malone,
Kilmeade, Athy, Co. Kildare

*Brian prepares for his annual trip to march with fellow
army veterans in the annual Easter Rising parade, his reflections
tinged by being only too aware that this trip for the
100th anniversary might be his last …*

H E REMEMBERED WHAT his father had once said of himself: that he was the sort of man who would handle old age very well, as he'd practised being old since he was very young. And now, Brian wondered if he would be as stoic as his father had been in his final years.

Brian loved to watch nature programmes on TV. He liked pink flamingos and their trait of standing on one leg in the lake. It reminded him of his own medical condition, in the sense that he had one foot in the grave. 78, he told the bathroom mirror. No lie, he breathed, wishing it was, by at least 20 years.

Would you look at that wrinkly oul puss. Is that really me? He thought. I don't feel that old inside.

He shaved, forcing himself not to notice the two green eyes with the yellowy whites looking back at him. The image of his father, they said. And he was indeed a carbon copy, right down to the maple birthmark under the lobe of his right ear.

According to his mother, he had his father's way of looking at you whenever he disapproved of how something was being done or had been said. His lips seemed to go in at one corner, like the air had been let out of them, and his eyes fell into a squint, like he was taking a good aim.

It was five a.m. And he had to be in Dublin for the Easter Parade by eight. He would be on his feet for the best part of the day, but it would be his last long walk anywhere and he would remember that when his feet and knees started to quake in protest.

It was an unspoken 'near' fact, between him and his daughter, that he would not see the 101st celebration of the Easter Rising. Brian Tolan would be part of history.

A knock to the door was followed by 'Dad?'

'Almost ready,' he said.

These days, since his fall, he knew that Louise worried about him being in the bathroom. A while back he'd cracked his head off the rim of the toilet bowl. Didn't need stitching or anything but for weeks he'd worn a black eye. MRI scan too, to make sure there was nothing dangerous lurking inside his head – and in the scanning they found his headstone date. A year...two... three at a push, they said. Ticking bomb, I am, he thought.

He lived alone: just him and his panic alarm hanging around his neck like a lazy hound. His carer came in two mornings a week, while Louise visited most of the other mornings. Or if not, she rang. People worrying about him he found most upsetting. That more so than the wrinkles, appeared to toll loudly how old and vulnerable he had become.

In the bedroom he had shared with Pauline for 40 years, he dressed in his army veteran slacks and jacket. Both of which the long mirror, on the inside of Pauline's wardrobe, announced were falling off him. Robust man he once was, with square shoulders and forearms like shanks of ham.

Briefly, he felt like giving way to the well of emotion that came of a sudden and unexpectedly. He sat to the edge of the bed and put his elbows on his knees, his head in his hands. His body was the ocean and his soul a message in a bottle, cast every which way in the storm.

Get a grip, he told himself, blinking back his tears.

He rose slowly, knees popping, and checked his medals were sitting properly across his blazer. Four with colourful miniature flags: Military Service, Congo, Cyprus and UN.

'You look very smart, Dad,' Louise said when he appeared before her in the sitting room.

His shoes were highly polished and his slacks and blazer pressed. He fixed his blue UN beret on his head. He'd had Louise buy it online – it was French made and a better fit than the UN standard issue. His medals he had sent to a soldier in Cathal Brugha barracks to be mounted on a single board.

'I've shrunk,' he said to her, bringing his tunic out from his tummy.

She said nothing. In the silence he looked up and caught the strain in her face that she moved on like a sky breeze did to clouds.

'We'll have it taken in,' she said.

'Hmmm … ,' he said, adding, 'the clocks moved forward an hour...'

She asked him what time he had to be in barracks to catch the bus to the city. He reckoned he must have already told her six times, if not more. He understood that they were talking merely to decorate the silences that would otherwise have been left hanging.

Louise dropped him at the pick-up point outside the barracks and asked if he was sure he'd be okay. He was staying in a Dublin hotel tonight, meeting up with former comrades who had come up for the parade from the country. Good laughs were squeezed from old memories and news too would be relayed, about who was ailing, who had gone since last year, the state of the army now as opposed to their day, the good and bad of it. Sing the song of their generation that was gradually slipping off the stage.

His daughter knew better than to ask him to spare himself the waiting around and marching and the late night frolics. This was a tradition deeply rooted. He was six when his father had brought him here and educated him about his own father, who had died in the GPO, killed by artillery fire.

It was a sad year of it, sad and terrible, for brother had killed brother, father and uncle. for different causes, dying not knowing the other was dead. Brian had always thought that a poignant tale. If he were to spin it further: the men had been twins. War did that, he thought, played such tricks, threw in some anomalies.

Hadn't he seen it out foreign. A fellow called Max Brennan had asked him to switch duty: he would do Sunday and Brian would fill in for him on Monday. Max died on the Sunday. War games is right, he thought.

Although he had tightened his belt to the last notch, he felt he could have done with piercing an extra hole in it. The slack needed apprehending. Must be a 30 waist now, he thought, down from a 36.

He moved past the military policeman on gate duty, and walked the margin of the square to the crowd of familiar faces standing in and around the flag carrier, Tankser Mullally. Talking and joking in the cold, waiting to hear the order to fall into formation. A stiff wind tore at apple blossoms beside a recently re-painted cannon. Pink petals on the ground reminded him of confetti and the flamingos in the zoo.

He detected the smell of cigarette smoke as he drew near to his colleagues, and counted in his mind how long it'd been since he'd quit smoking. Ten years ... no eleven.

Handshakes and smiles. Some had aged badly since last year, and they no doubt thought likewise of him. Tankser and he had served together in Cyprus, in administration roles at the UN base in Nicosia, and had brought along their families for the last six months.

Tankser handed the flag over to another man and said to Brian, 'We've time for a quick cuppa in the Mess.'

Brian had eaten a good breakfast, by his usual standards, and didn't want tea, not wanting to risk getting caught short during the 4 kilometre parade; and they could be waiting for a long while too.

Still, he could perhaps pierce his trouser belt. He didn't like its looseness.

Tankser walked with his torso leaning forward, listing off the new ailments he'd acquired since last Easter and repeated a couple of old ones too, that had since worsened. He'd lost his thick moustache and the black circles under his eyes signalled his pain.

Inside the Mess, Tankser poured tea into cups and picked a digestive biscuit from a paper plate.

Borrowing a corkscrew from behind the bar, Brian excused himself. It wasn't as easy a job as he'd imagined. The belt leather was tough, but he managed to create an eyelet and another also.

He joined Tankser at a table, sat on a low cushioned stool opposite him, and added milk to tea he did not intend to drink.

'One hundred years,' Tankser said in a low voice.

'Yes...' Brian acknowledged.

From where they were sitting they could see the barrack square through the narrow window. Brian glanced at his watch and said, 'We've got five minutes.'

Tankser said, rubbing the back of his hand, 'I was talking to Louise ... she rang me to ask if I'd keep an eye on you ...'

'Did she now?'

Tankser nodded, 'She did. I'm saying ... you don't have to push yourself, Brian ... you can wait here and watch the parade on the telly. Get a cab to the hotel later. It's a plan, yeah?'

Silence.

Tankser sighed.

'I have to do this,' Brian said, 'you know there's a family connection to the occasion and every year I come to the City, I feel that I'm bringing closure to something. That there's a healing taking place.'

To the window, Tankser said, 'And after you ... ?'

Brian said quickly, 'That'll be for Louise to decide. She thinks its tripe, the whole military thing.'

'There's a stir,' Tankser said, getting to his feet.

Brian felt a weakness come over him as he stood, light-headedness too. Tankser said quietly, 'Are you okay?'

'Fine... I was just thinking about the pink flamingos in the zoo...'

'Yeah...?'

Above his word came the sounds of a platoon marching to a low roll drum.

'I think that's how we have to be ... like them,' Brian said.

'Like a pink bird?' Tankser said, as they rejoined their group, re-taking the flag.

'Keep one leg out of the water, i.e. the grave, for as long as possible,' Brian explained, but feeling that he wasn't making a good fist of explaining.

Tankser smiled, shook his head and said, 'You always had a peculiar way of looking at things.'

'Do you think?' Brian said, as they made to form up in line.

'Pink birds how are ya,' Tankser said; 'one foot in a watery grave, looking on at the world.'

They began to march, and he felt as though he was running on empty after less than ten minutes marching. When they paused, he felt the cold wind drying his perspiration. The soles of his feet ached and so too his shins. Concentrated on the two brothers on opposing sides – his grandfather, a grand uncle – each step he took, he thought, was one towards a reconciliation, towards a complete and full understanding that no one escapes suffering in war-time.

The next day Louise was quiet in the car on the way home after collecting him at the hotel.

'Did you watch the parade on the telly?' he said when they had gotten onto the M50, and had slowed on entering heavy traffic.

'A little of it,' she replied.

'It's not for the glory, Louise – it's to remember, to pay respect. That's all we do,' he said.

'You don't need a gun to pay your respects,' she snapped.

'I wasn't carrying a weapon.'

'You know what I mean, Dad.'

'I'll leave you my medals,' he said, on a cough.

She glanced across at him and said smiling, 'I'll flog them.'

'You'll keep the blue beret though?'

'I might.'

Then he smoothed over their differences and spoke of Tankser and others, re-telling stories she would have heard before. God, my legs, he thought, the veins are after tying themselves into knots. He stretched the worse leg of the pair. Ah, better.

Noticing his grimace, Louise said, 'Dad, are you okay?'
'I am. God I am. I'm just changing legs.'

Martin Malone is the author of 10 books, several radio plays and a stage play. His writings have won many literary awards and competitions, including the Ireland's Own *Short Story Competiton,* RTE's Francis MacManus Short Story Award, *the Killarney 250 International Short Story Prize, and the inaugural Cecil Day Lewis Literary Bursary Award. Twenty of his short stories have been broadcast on RTE and BBC radio. A former soldier with the Irish army, he has served six tours of duty in the Middle East, in Lebanon and Iraq. He is currently teaching English to war refugees from Iraq and Syria.*

Sammy

By Anthony Rooney,
Kimmage, Dublin

Sammy lived near my mother in sheltered accommodation. He kept himself to himself and little was known of his early life and few attended his funeral. Hoping to trace next of kin, we had a look through his meagre possessions …

A WEEK AFTER Sammy's funeral I received a call from my mother seeking my advice. Before going into hospital for his operation, Sammy had entrusted the key of his flat to her. On his death my mother had contacted the Council; they arranged for a social worker to call and collect the keys within the next few days, but she was anxious to search the flat in the hope of finding his next of kin.

Sammy had been her next door neighbour, in sheltered accommodation in Finglas, but not once in the fifteen years he'd lived there had he ever mentioned friends or family. He'd once confided in a neighbour that he'd worked on the railways before an accident had left him partly disabled with a bad limp.

He was of medium size, with a darkish, swarthy complexion and a head of black, unruly hair that was striking in a man in his mid-sixties. He spoke with a soft country accent. Some said he was from Cork but, though courteous to all, he kept his business to himself.

Sometimes, when visiting my mother, I'd see him passing; he'd exchange a few words about the weather but, unlike the other old folk, never stopped to talk. Despite his aloofness, my mother spoke well of him and described him as a proper gentleman. Sometimes, when he wasn't too well, she'd fetch his messages from the village, but other than that he kept pretty much to himself.

I called out to my mother on a Saturday morning. Over a cup of tea she told me of Sammy's funeral, how most of the old folk had attended the church, but only six people had followed the remains to the cemetery. After she'd finished her account, I suggested we look through Sammy's flat and see if we could find anything of interest.

Sheltered accommodation consists of two types of flats: a single tenant has one room, a sort of bed/sitter, with a small scullery for cooking and a shower and toilet; couples are given two rooms.

My mother opened the door and we stepped into Sammy's flat. It was sparsely furnished – a single bed with two pillows and a crumpled duvet lying at one end; a small drop leaf table, on it a teapot, cup and saucer with two small plates, all unwashed.

There was a fairly large chest of drawers containing an assortment of clothing, a sagging armchair, two wooden chairs and a television on a small table. In the small scullery there was a wall press containing a half full packet of cereal, but what surprised us was the amount of canned food – there were tins of tuna, salmon and sardines.

Beside the sink unit was a small fridge in which was a half used carton of milk, a packet of cheese and a bottle of Seven Up. In a wall press we found a carry bag, under it was a biscuit tin; I lifted it onto the table. Inside was a loose collection of photographs. 'Now we're getting somewhere,' I said.

As we sifted through the photographs my mother held one up, 'This looks like his family.' It showed a boy about eight years old, and a girl a few years older, sitting on either side of their mother, the father standing behind them. They stared at the camera with the solemn, unsmiling faces, characteristic of that time.

There were several school photographs, two of them showing the young Sammy posing proudly as a member of the school football team. Most interesting of all was a photograph of Sammy and a pretty young girl, both sporting rosettes in their lapels, crossing O'Connell Bridge. We found another snap of the same girl, looking shy and beautiful, in a studio setting.

None of the snaps had details of dates or places, which was rather frustrating. At the bottom of the tin was a piece of red velvet; we unwrapped it and found a cheap brooch. It was a butterfly studded with green and red glass beads. 'It could have been his mother's,' I suggested.

My mother shook her head, 'No, older women don't wear brooches like that; this belonged to his girl, whatever her name was.'

The tin revealed no more secrets, nor indeed the rest of the flat; it seemed Sammy was to be as reticent in death as he'd been in life. 'What should we do with them?' my mother asked.

'If we leave them, the council workers will throw them out,' I said.

'I'll hold them for a while, somebody might call,' she said, returning the snaps to the tin.

It struck me how elusive happiness can sometimes be; in a few days the council workers would arrive, Sammy's meagre possessions would barely fill their skip. The flat would be scrubbed, cleaned and decorated and a new tenant installed. He was obviously a simple man; no paintings adorned his walls, there were no book-lined shelves to indicate his tastes, or lack of them, and yet, like all of us, he must have had his dreams.

Perhaps he dreamed of glory on the playing field, of wearing the red jersey of his county and winning the acclaim and admiration of his fellows. Maybe he dreamed of love and happiness with the beautiful girl in his photographs; clearly such dreams had not come true. Had she died? Emigrated? Or found happiness with another?

Whatever the reason, Sammy's life had led him to live out his closing years among those he barely knew, or even cared to know.

How sad that there should be none to mourn his death; that his passing should be as unnoticed as his brief and lonely life.

'Are you ready?' my mother asked.

I nodded. She lifted the biscuit tin and I followed her out the door.

Anthony Rooney is a retired Irish Rail worker with a grown up family, grandchildren and a great grandchild. He is a member of Pearse Street Creative Writers' Group. He began writing in his sixties and had two plays broadcast on RTÉ as part of the P.J. O'Connor competition.

Blame it on Bullet

By Thomas F. Morgan,
Glasheen, Cork

*A naïve young schoolboy is introduced to the intricacies and
excitement of the horse racing and betting world when he is
told about 'a good thing', the information coming 'straight
from the horse's mouth'. What could go wrong?*

BULLET WAS THE class act in our school. While we
were all more or less the same age he always seemed
years older. Because he seemed so streetwise and older
we sensed a hint of danger about him which led to his nickname,
Bullet. It was known that he smoked cigarettes, he shaved once
a week and even had a girlfriend. This was a guy who knew
the ways of the world. Like the rest of my classmates I was
very much in awe of Bullet and all his pronouncements on life
and how to live it were accepted without question.

One Saturday morning I bumped into Bullet in town. He
called me aside with a conspiratorial wave of the hand. He
whispered into my ear that he knew about a 'good thing'.
I tried to maintain a cool and knowing exterior while trying
to decipher exactly what he meant by this cryptic statement.
He obviously gleaned that I had no idea what he was talking
about. Aware that I led a sheltered life, but taking pity on
my ignorance he explained what it was all about.

It turned out that his sister's best friend had a second cousin
who had a friend who worked as a stable lad for a well-

known trainer named Hurley. Information had been received through this reliable route that a horse which was due to run the following Saturday in Ballinrobe was 'past the post' and Bullet explained that this information had come 'straight from the horse's mouth'.

I was not to reveal this to a single person. If I did I would suffer unexplained consequences. He told me I should 'get on early and often'. I immediately realised that this was priceless information but I was at a loss as to how to translate it into a cash profit. However, my embarrassment at my level of ignorance was only exceeded by my greed so I asked Bullet how I could use this information for personal gain.

From the way he explained it there were really no complications. All I had to do was to make my way to a bookies office the following Saturday, place a bet on the horse in question and after it had won the race the bookie would multiply my stake by the odds of the winner and pay me out there and then. He then whispered the name of the winner in my ear – Hurricane Hilda.

The following week was spent accumulating my stake money by fair means and foul. This included secretly extracting money from my sister's piggy bank. This was easily justified by the fact that it was guaranteed to be returned after Hilda had obliged. By the following Saturday I had managed to get together the princely sum of £2. Having been told that there was a bookie located on South Main Street I made sure to be at the premises in plenty of time for the race, which was due off at two o'clock.

When I arrived there I have to say that I was impressed by the large sign on the door which read Honest Jem Malone – Turf Accountant. The sign told me that not only could that man be trusted to pay me out but he also seemed to hold professional qualifications.

I eagerly opened the front door which led to a steep flight of steps down to a basement behind another door. As the noise of the traffic faded with my descent I could hear an increasing cacophony of noise coming from behind the door which I slowly opened to reveal a netherworld which I had been blissfully unaware of until that fateful day.

As the door opened I was hit by a wave of thick cigarette smoke which emanated from every member of this all-male world. As I tried to make out what was happening through this thick gloom, a range of startling sights met my eye. Behind the counter was an enormous, fat man wearing a dirty shirt and braces who kept shouting at no one in particular to 'get on before they're off'.

An old fellow in the corner, who no doubt had spent the morning in one of the local early houses, was asleep with his head resting on a table using a paper entitled '*The Sporting Life*' as a pillow. All the walls in the room were decorated with sheets of paper which were covered in hieroglyphics which were being studied with great purpose by throngs of fellows called punters. In the corner a tannoy gave out a non-stop incomprehensible babble.

One man stood in the middle of the room staring at the tannoy and as the noise from the tannoy began to increase in volume this seemed to have a marked effect on his physical state. His face began to turn first red and then purple. Sweat began to run down his forehead and the veins on his neck began to bulge in a frightening manner.

It appeared that this man was succumbing to some serious physical or mental disorder. He began to rock back and forth on his feet and screaming nonsensical statements like 'get up ya daisy', 'come on my son' and 'get him home'. What was amazing about this scene was that everyone else in the room was completely oblivious to this poor man's plight and gave no impression of concern about his well-being.

Just when I thought I was about to witness his mortal end the noise from the tannoy stopped and he suddenly took on a completely normal demeanour as he hurled a piece of paper across the room which bounced off the drunk's head.

With all this excitement over, I began to look at the numerous papers on the wall realising that I could find the reference to Hurricane Hilda's race. I knew it was in Ballinrobe but beyond that I had no inkling as to how to place a bet. It was then that the Artist spotted me and obviously took pity on me. He was sitting in the corner reading a copy of the *Sporting Life* with a pencil strategically placed over his right ear and a pair of glasses perched halfway up his nose.

He asked if he could assist me in any way and when I mentioned the name of the horse he quickly drew the glasses up over his eyes and made a beeline for a paper on a nearby wall. He stared intently at the paper for about half a minute then returned to his seat and with a voice of authority said to me, 'Hanly up for Hurley, keep your money in your pocket'.

I tried to react in a calm, knowing fashion but my total incomprehension as to what he actually meant must have been obvious because he then gave me a sympathetic explanation of what was about to happen in Ballinrobe.

He told me that among punters the jockey named Hanly who was up on Hurricane Hilda was known by experienced punters as Handbrake Hanly due to his skill at stopping horses from winning. It was claimed that he could have stopped Arkle in a two horse race without coming to the attention of the stewards.

His notorious reputation for crookery was only exceeded by the trainer, Hurley, who specialised in giving out false tips on his horses to mug punters and then ensuring that the horse would lose by putting up Hanly with careful instructions to come in at the rear end of every other horse in the race.

He would then produce the same horse at a later date with another jockey up and the horse would invariably win at a big price, no doubt because the horse would not be weighed down by a flood of money on its back, apart that is from the money put on by Hurley himself.

The Artist displayed such in-depth knowledge and spoke with such authority that I immediately decided to take his advice. His prediction about the race was absolutely true and the horse trailed in second last in the field of twenty.

While my experience that day should have acted as a warning to steer clear of punting and everything to do with it, the reality is that it had the opposite effect on me. I was fascinated and challenged by this world of risk-takers and thirty years later I am still learning lessons about the punting game, some more costly than others. Enter this world at your peril.

Tom Morgan, originally from Cork City, has a B.A. in English and History. He now resides in Dublin and works as a Civil Servant. Over the years he has written short stories as a pastime. His partner, Gabrielle Nic Reamoinn, works as a publishers' agent. This short story is the first time he has ever submitted material for publication.

Fortune Telling for Mother Teresa

By Elizabeth Johnson,
Wicklow

Having heard about Mother Teresa and her work as a teenager,
I was inspired to raise funds to assist her and adopted a rather
incongruous method for doing so ...

IT WAS SHORTLY after the Stardust tragedy in 1981, when 48 young people lost their lives in a nightclub fire, so people paid attention to the church warden when he told them that the church could not accommodate any more people than the Fire Safety Regulations allowed. A tannoy system had been set up outside so that those on the street could hear a guest of honour speak.

I was home on holiday from the UK, where I lived at the time, when my friend Eithne told me that Mother Teresa would be speaking in Whitefriar Street Church in Dublin that evening. She knew that I admired the nun and recommended that I be there around 5.30 p.m. as a huge crowd was expected.

I first heard of Mother Teresa when I was a teenager. In the Letters to the Editor section of one of the national daily newspapers a lady had written about a visit she made to Calcutta where she had chanced upon the work of the former Loreto nun.

She invited people to write to her for more information if they were interested in helping. At the time Mother Teresa

71

was unknown outside India. I immediately wrote to the lady and received a great deal of information by return. As I was still a schoolgirl, she recommended that I become a Co-Worker of the Missionaries of Charity, Mother Teresa's community, which meant praying and reading the regular newsletters sent to me.

As soon as I began to work, I tried to think of a ways to raise funds for Mother Teresa and her nuns who were caring for the 'poorest of the poor' in The Third World. At the time fortune-telling was very popular among my peer group and my friends and I would often go to visit Gypsy Lee or some other so-called 'psychic'.

Some of my friends took fortune-telling very seriously while others like me saw it as nothing more than a bit of fun. It was always a good night out, however, as we would end up in a Wimpy Bar laughing about our 'future prospects'. That was how I got the idea for fundraising.

I began to read books on fortune-telling and soon learned how to read the Tarot Cards, the palms and the handwriting. Before long I was inundated with requests from my friends and fellow workers to read their fortune. I made it very clear to everyone that I had no psychic powers but just read the cards in the order in which they fell.

Within a short time, my reputation as a fortune-teller grew and my appointment book for readings was full. My lunch 'hour' got shorter every day as more and more people came to me for readings. I charged no fee but asked for a small donation and I lodged the money raised in a bank in Dublin where a charges-free account had been set up in the name of The Missionaries of Charity.

On arrival at Whitefriar Street that evening, the church was already half-full but I managed to get a seat near the front. At 7.30 p.m. a priest came out onto the altar and spoke to the congregation for a few minutes before he introduced the elderly nun.

Mother Teresa was a tiny woman, slightly stooped, with a smile that radiated inner peace. Dressed in a simple white sari with blue trimming, her face was heavily lined from years of working among the poor in the searing Indian heat. She arrived on the altar accompanied by another nun, who stood silently in the background.

Using a microphone, she slowly began to speak. I was immediately impressed by her gentle voice, the brevity of her sentences and the hushed silence of the congregation. I suddenly found myself comparing her to another well-known woman at the time, Maggie Thatcher, the British Prime Minister.

Having lived under this domineering woman's leadership since 1979, I was tired of hearing her loud demanding voice and bullying tone. The contrast between the two women was unbelievable. Mother Teresa spoke very quietly in short sentences of not more than ten words during which time you could hear a pin drop.

I listened entranced as the diminutive nun told us about the work of her community in the 'Home for the Dying', with the lepers and with the abandoned children. I was simply spellbound by her simple words and message.

Mother Teresa left the altar that evening to thunderous applause, something I had never before heard in a church. Many people stood on their seats in order to get a better view as she left the altar. Seeing Mother Teresa (now Saint Teresa) in person that evening was a truly wonderful experience and one I will never forget.

Elizabeth Johnson was born in Ireland in the late forties and grew up on the east coast. She studied Literature at London University, Frankfurt University and later at Oxford University. She originally began writing in order to pay her university fees. She has been writing articles and short stories for newspapers and magazines for many years. She won first prize in the Ireland's Own *writing competition in 2013 and this is her fifth anthology appearance. She returned to Ireland a few years ago and currently resides in Co. Wicklow.*

Moment of Truth

By Deirdre Comiskey,
Beaumont Woods, Dublin

Kathleen had her life mapped out ahead of her as she proudly graduated with her law degree; she knew just what she wanted to do. But then she met Brian and all her plans went out the window and her life was nothing like she had planned ...

KATHLEEN SHOULD NOT be here. Not in this house, not living this life, not in this country. This was never her plan. From an early age she had known very clearly what she did want and had planned carefully how she would achieve it. Focused. That was the word her friends used when they described her.

Well at least that was the case until the pivotal moment in her life when she had met Brian and had without further thought thrown all her carefully laid plans out the window. That was ten years ago.

Fresh out of college in Dublin with her first class honours law degree, the world was her oyster. Her mind raced back to her graduation ceremony in UCD that September – the excitement of strutting into the hall in her cap and gown, the proud smiles of her mother and father as they watched their precious only child, the first to go to college in their family, as she was conferred with a Bachelor of Civil Law.

She knew their hands were sore with clapping so hard for her as she sailed back to her seat, the sense of achievement

75

filling her with excitement. She could do anything now, go anywhere, and be whoever she wanted to be.

The telephone made her jump and she raced to answer it fearing the worst. It was only someone wanting to discuss alternative energy suppliers with her. It wasn't their day. It wasn't her day. In fact, she wished it was any day but today.

She made another cup of strong coffee and sat down remembering how she had met Brian working in a big city law firm in London. Straight from college, she was a newbie and Brian was assigned to be her 'buddy', a practice the firm had developed for integrating the interns.

She was waiting in reception on her first day when a well groomed guy in his late twenties, with dark auburn wavy hair and navy blue eyes, strode over to her. Tall and deeply tanned he smiled at her. Holding out his hand, he introduced himself, explaining that he would take care of her – she hoped he meant for the rest of her life.

Their romance wasn't so much a whirlwind as a hurricane. It raced along with such an intensity friends said it could never be sustained.

Within two months he had begged her to marry him and, encased in the dreamy world of romance, she had agreed without even thinking about the practical consequences. She would listen to no one, not her parents who argued she was too young, she had not given herself a chance to enjoy life; or her friends who took her to task over committing herself to the first guy she had allowed herself to get serious about.

Within six months of starting her career she was married and expecting her daughter. Her mother cried when she heard. They were not tears of joy but of sadness because she was afraid her daughter had wasted the precious opportunities she had been given and would regret for her life.

Three more children followed in quick succession and Kathleen had to admit that she would never qualify as a solicitor. The cost of childcare meant that giving up work to be a full-time mother was her only option. Brian worked hard to make ends meet but he was called upon to work at all hours of the day and night as he moved his way up the corporate ladder.

Kathleen settled with him in Wimbledon and soon the years swept by in a haze of sleepless nights with the babies, busy school runs as they got older and the humdrum of food shopping and housekeeping that was a chore but had to be done. Brian was now 39 and, facing his 40th birthday, he was finally offered a full partnership in the firm, a reward for the dedication he had shown to the job. He was still handsome, his auburn hair now tinged with the first signs of maturing grey, and frown lines spelt out the years of concentration on his forehead.

Kathleen looked at her reflection in the mirror. She had to admit that at 33 she looked her age. Being responsible for four little people who depended on you to feed and clothe and love them daily brought a maturity to her that her close friends hadn't yet found.

Her relationship with her mother had never recovered from the shock caused by her abandonment of her career and life goals. Brian, too, had been affected by their decisions. She knew he felt deeply guilty that she had to give up her career to raise their family. Try as she would to convince him other-wise, he felt she secretly resented the choices she had made because of him.

She tried to think back before the children, before Brian. What was it she had wanted so badly? What was it she had missed out on? What had her friends got that she hadn't?

Growing up she had pictured herself as a human rights lawyer defending the disenfranchised, the poor, the people with no voices. She would study hard, get her law degree and qualify as a solicitor, then look for a reputable charity and start to build the experience she would need to fulfil her dreams. Marriage was not high on her agenda and the truth was, as a teenager she never thought much about having a family.

No, hers was a nobler calling, She would make a difference to humanity, she would change things for the better. She planned on living in London while she qualified and returning to her hometown of Killarney with its beautiful National Park and rugged coastline which was ever dear to her heart. She would base herself there near her parents. As an only child, she wanted to be a support for her mother and father and to see them as often as she could while flying abroad to undertake her international work.

A big tear rolled down her cheek, splashing into her cup. She missed her mother so much, missed the closeness they once had, missed the pride in her mother's eyes as she looked at her. Her mother visited a couple of times a year and Kathleen tried to make as many trips to Killarney as she could. But somehow they could never get back to the way it used to be.

Her father and Brian got on well, discussing sports and politics but they didn't understand the gulf she felt between herself and her mum. If only she and Brian could have moved back to Killarney. There was no hope now that he had finally been made a partner. She was in Wimbledon and in Wimbledon she would stay, at least if her worst fears didn't materialise.

Afraid. She realised that she had been afraid for the last six months. Ever since Brian had taken to disappearing off on business trips and was secretive about his destinations. 'Confidential,' he had said, not something he could tell her.

Did he really think she was that big of a fool? It was obvious to her that there was someone else in his life.

He had taken to making late night calls on his mobile and when she asked who he was speaking to he had made random excuses about following up with clients out of hours. He had been away this last week and had said he wanted to speak about something very important with her on his return.

Important. That could only mean one thing couldn't it? He had finally decided to leave her. He was seeing someone else, the reason for the business trips and late night calls. It was an old story surely, one she had heard many times from friends. And yet she could not really find it in her heart to believe it. She still loved Brian deeply and up to a few months ago was convinced he felt the same despite their ups and downs.

It never rains but it pours her Gran used to say and she was right. Kathleen had just had a call from her father an hour ago saying her mum was in the hospital with a fractured leg, having tripped on her way to Mass and was having it set in the local hospital under anaesthetic. Kathleen was sick with worry and willing the phone to ring and for her father to say her mother was out of the operation and in recovery.

She heard the key in the lock as Brian arrived home. Throwing his bag in the hall he wandered into the kitchen. Seeing her white tear-stained face he flung his arms around Kathleen and she, relieved to have him home and yet scared to hear his news, told him between sobs about her mum. He made her a fresh cup of tea and gently took her hand in his.

'Kathleen,' he said in a low voice 'there is something you should know.' Ashen-faced she could barely look at him and tried to speak but nothing would come out.

'Kathleen, I have always, always regretted the way I rushed you into marriage,' he began. Oh no, he regretted their marriage. This was it. It was really over. She needed to face it.

Brian saw the shock on her face and continued gently: 'Honey you have sacrificed so much for me and the children and I know I haven't been here when I should have been to give you support. I know you have had a hard time away from your home and your family, especially your mother, and that you never had the chance to reach your full career potential because of my selfishness.

'Well I have been thinking and planning and I have something amazing to tell you. This partnership I have been offered is based in Ireland. I have been asked to set up a branch of our office in Cork. The trips I have been making have been to assess the potential and find suitable premises. I didn't want to tell you in case it fell through but I have just sealed the deal.

'I have also been looking for a temporary house for us until we can choose our new forever home together. That can be in Killarney if you want to be near your mother, or anywhere else you want my darling, because I will do whatever I can to make up to you for all that you have had to give up because of me.

'I have also made enquiries with the Law Society in Dublin and you can enrol to continue your studies if that's what you want and take up an apprenticeship at our new branch in Cork. The children are in school most of the day, and with my new position I can afford for us to have a nanny if you think we need one. Darling, please say something.'

Kathleen's brain was racing. trying to make sense of what Brian had just said. He wasn't leaving her? There was no one else. He still loved her! He loved her and he was willing to move to Ireland for her. She would be near her dear mum and dad, They would rebuild their bond. There was time. There was still plenty of time. Time for her Mum to truly get to know the wonderful man she had married and for her children to finally have their grandparents in their lives.

That is if her Mum survived the operation.

She nearly jumped out of her skin as her mobile screeched on the table. 'Kathleen, it's your dad. Mum is fine. She's in the recovery room. What did you say? You're coming home. For a visit. For good? Really darling girl? Oh Kathleen that's grand. It's really grand – the best present you could ever give to us. Just wait until I tell your Mum. Sure she will think she has died and gone to Heaven'.

Deirdre Comiskey lives in Dublin with her husband Matt and Teddy, their dog. A chartered accountant by profession but a story teller at heart, Deirdre was a finalist in the Ireland AM Christmas Short Story Competition 2014. She has had the pleasure of seeing her stories published in Ireland's Own *and is working on her first novel.*

The Day the Sheep Came to Town

By Jane Flood,
Ballon, Co. Carlow

The day the sheep had to be gathered for inspection and counting 'by the Man from the Department' to qualify for the new Common Market subsidies turned into a festival occasion in some places ...

AFTER IRELAND JOINED the EEC in 1973 rural communities experienced a huge amount of change in a relatively short space of time. Farm modernisation, improved infrastructure and large scale use of machinery all had a part to play. Small holders in disadvantaged areas were targeted to be helped; farmers were introduced to a new and very welcome concept, the subsidy or headage payment.

The village farmers would bring their flocks down to be inspected and counted by the man from the department who would then write up his report and money would be allocated accordingly. The Department of Agriculture and Fisheries, as it was known at that time, wasn't the well-oiled machine that it is now and reflected a society that was emerging blinking into the light of the shiny new Europe.

The Sheep Subsidy Day, as it was known in these parts, was a veritable festival of sheep. The big field beside the church would be prepared for days beforehand. Old gates, pallets and stakes would be brought down and makeshift pens would be constructed against the graveyard wall. The local pub would stock up on drink in anticipation of a larger crowd than usual.

The sheep would be gathered and brought down off the mountain in preparation for their big day out. Sheep were 'raddled' to distinguish the flocks from each other. A marking system using red or blue initials would be used.

The sheep would be driven down early on the morning of the subsidy check, often over two or three miles. Help was needed to stand in laneways and open gateways. We would bring our own sheep down early and then go back and help out with other flocks as needed.

This would continue through the morning and it was hard work, requiring a lot of running to and fro among sheep that didn't know what was going on. By mid-morning most of the flocks would be down and the serious work could begin.

We would await the arrival of Tim, the man from the department, or the grant man as he was more commonly known. He would arrive in his shiny motor car. He was a tall, imposing looking fellow. He wore slacks and a brightly coloured shirt, standing out among the men's long grey coats, collarless shirts and hob nailed boots.

His all-important book would be sticking out of the back pocket of his slacks. He enjoyed his work and understood his power but he had one fatal flaw that they had discovered and would play to the hilt.

Between one and two o'clock they would break for dinner and head down to the local pub for refreshments. There would be sandwiches, biscuits and minerals on offer. But in the bar, large bottles and half whiskies were the order of the day. The grant man would have drink after drink put in front of him from grateful men looking forward to their big pay day, and he reasoned that it would be rude not to drink them all.

When Tim came back from dinner he was a different man. It is not easy to count moving sheep at the best of times and some less-than-honest souls would suggest a number greatly in excess of the actual figure and Tim would be in no mood or condition to argue. He had quite a bit of work to get through and he would put on his glasses and stare at his book with a worried look.

He would not be the only casualty that day; men who would not normally drink much would give in to the festive atmosphere with predictable results. They would get so under the weather that they wouldn't be able to bring the flock home, or they would try, and lose half of them.

The dutiful and sensible men who had brought their flocks home would tut tut next morning as they passed by and their more adventurous neighbour's flock remained penned in the deserted field, the owner having outdone himself in the festivities. Down in the local hostelry, the day would be gone over in detail with the grant man safely asleep on the counter. As one grateful farmer would offer us a pound for our help that morning, another would go two pounds not to be seen to be outdone in generosity. The younger people would go home stiff and sore from all the running but with pockets full of crumpled pound notes.

Over forty years later, most of these men are on the far side of that graveyard wall having gone to their eternal reward. They were all imbued with great optimism about the Common Market; what they would make of it all we can only wonder.

Jane Flood is married to Mick and they have seven daughters. She has written for her local Ballon-Rathoe Chronicle *and had a short story in the* Carlow Nationalist *newspaper. This is her first time to be published in a full scale book. She is a member of John McKenna's Library Writers Group which meets monthly in Carlow.*

Rock-a-Bye

By Joe Buckley,
Maynooth, Co. Kildare

The young girl survived a car crash that claimed the lives of her parents. She is deeply traumatised and refuses all communication with those around her, even her beloved grandmother who is at her wits end about what to do ...

THE NINE-year-old girl descended the stairs slowly, clutching the palm-polished banister with her left hand. Her long russet hair was uncombed and hung tiredly down her faded red nightie. The straps of her sandals flapped with each step. At the bottom of the stairs she paused, eyeing the half-open kitchen door, listening for a moment to a woman speaking importantly on the radio. Then she slid through the doorway.

The grandmother stood at the counter slicing a brown loaf. Her silver hair was fixed in a bun behind her head, her light blue dress dotted with small white flowers. The apron, tied behind her back with string, was navy blue.

Hearing the chair legs scraping on the flags, she turned. Her lips formed a smile, but her grey-blue eyes were sad. The girl sat on the edge of the chair by the table, rocking lightly, her fists clenched between her knees.

'Ah, there you are, alannah,' the woman said. 'You crept in like a fairy on me.' The girl's grave eyes fixed on the granny's face, but she didn't speak. One might say that the eyes were looking, but not seeing.

'You can go to the rocking chair after breakfast,' the grand-mother said. As she passed behind the girl, her raised hand hovered over the russet hair, but she didn't touch. 'I'm putting strawberry jam on the bread the way you like it. And if the tea's too cold, just tell, just let me know.'

As the woman placed a plate on the table, the telephone jang-led in the hall. She dusted her hands on her apron and went to answer it.

'Ah, Helen, I thought you'd ring alright.' The grandmother's eyes watched the kitchen door as she listened. 'She's just up.' A pause. 'Not a lot. But at least she's nibbling.' She listened again. 'No, not a word. She just sits there looking. I can't tell what's going on in her little head. I don't know if she'll ever get over it.' Another pause. 'Yes, she has another appointment this morning. For all the good it does.' She shrugged. 'But I suppose they know best. Alright. See you at seven.'

When the grandmother re-entered the kitchen, the girl was in the rocking chair by the range, her legs tucked under her, her arms clutching one another. 'Will you not have tea, pet?' the woman asked softly. The girl stared at her, but made no response. The woman studied the half-eaten slice of bread and jam and sighed.

It was four weeks now since the funerals. To the grandmother it seemed like four months – four months of grieving for a daughter and a son-in-law. Her body was weary from lack of sleep. The nightmare of being woken by that strident ringing of the doorbell had left her fearful of sleep.

Moreover, she had trained herself to listen for every creak of the old bed springs in the next room, for every cough and sigh in the stillness of the night. At times she sat upright in her bed, her ear cocked, yearning for a sob that would break the long silence and send her hurrying to the child's side. But always it was the howl of a distant dog or a dawn bleat from a sheep in the paddock. It was as if the soul had been stolen from the girl, as if there were only emptiness inside her.

The girl had been in the car, miraculously fastened by the back seat belt. She'd lain unnoticed as the busy firemen strained the crushed metal to release her parents' bodies. At the end, a fireman had discovered her shivering and silent in the blackness of the back seat. And silent the girl had remained in the hospital, even in the face of the kindly nurses.

There was no comforting her. She shrank from every human touch, detaching herself gently but firmly from all attempted embrace. She obeyed all the grandmother's instructions in silence. She ate little and she refused to get into the car. She spent hours in the rocking chair, making her delicate body fit into the smallest space possible, rocking imperceptibly, as if unable to muster the energy to set it in proper motion.

Lately, though, the grandmother had felt the girl's eyes upon her as she moved about the kitchen. There was something so accusing in the intensity of the girl's gaze that the woman felt a sense of guilt creep over her, as if somehow she were responsible for the loss of the girl's parents. This morning was no different and the woman became so self-conscious that, after she'd tidied things away, she fled upstairs to make the beds. She was relieved when the church clock struck the hour and it was time to dress the girl and go for the train.

On the train, the girl sat by the window, her eyes fixed on the floor. In the clinic waiting room the woman and child sat side-by-side waiting for the receptionist to call them. The grandmother flicked through a magazine, keeping the pages lowered so that the girl might see the bright dresses on show there.

The psychiatrist, a humped man with thinning black hair, greeted the pair wearily as they entered his room. He asked the girl questions. Her grave eyes rested on his face, but she made no reply. His eyes invited the grandmother to speak. She looked at the girl and back at him. She had nothing to say.

'Alright, Aoife,' he said, rising from his chair. 'I have another little puzzle for you today. Can you come over to the table and I'll show you.'

The girl slid off her chair and followed to the table by the window. He explained the puzzle, left a pen beside her hand and came back to sit with the grandmother.

'Well, has she said anything?'

The woman shook her head. 'Not a word, doctor. There's no change. Except ...'

'Except?'

'Except she watches me. Every time I come into the kitchen she watches me like a hawk. It's like she's blaming me for what happened. Or it's like, it's like she wants me to do something, something simple – a simple thing that will break the spell, but I don't know what it is. Can you not think of *anything*, doctor?'

'Her friends, do they live close by?'

She shook her head. 'They're all back in Castletown, doctor. I could take her back for a few days, but it would be hard for her in the house. She's not ready for that yet.'

Later, after the doctor had studied the few markings the girl had made on the paper and arranged for another appointment, the grandmother took the girl back to the station. As they passed a shop she asked the girl if she would like sweets, but the girl declined.

Helpless, the grandmother felt a surge of rage. What was that bloody doctor doing anyway? Did he think that she could cure the girl all by herself? On the train, she stared down at the girl sitting upright in the window seat. She wanted to catch her and shake her, even hurt her, until she spoke. Even if she cried it would be better than this awful silence.

A bearded man with a white cane and a tan-coloured Labrador dog on a lead felt his way into the seat opposite her. The dog stood in the space in front of the girl. 'Sit, Prince. Sit,' the man said. The dog sat.

The girl looked at the dog and shifted her knees towards the wall of the carriage. She folded herself more tightly within her arms.

'Sit, Prince,' the man repeated. Behind his tinted glasses his eyes darted convulsively up under his bushy black eyebrows.

The dog settled patiently as dogs do. It opened its mouth and the lip of its pink tongue hung over its teeth. Its eyes rested momentarily on the face of the woman and of the girl.

The grandmother stowed the tickets in the zip pocket of her handbag. When next she looked, the dog had its head tilted to one side, its right ear cocked and its eyes fixed on the face of the girl.

'He likes you,' the grandmother whispered.

'Is the dog alright?' the blind man asked.

'No. No, he's grand,' the grandmother said. From the corner of her eye she saw that the girl was looking at the dog. The dog tilted its head to the other side but it still kept its eyes on the girl's face. Time stretched out.

Then, unbidden, the dog leaned forward and placed its head gently on the girl's knees, its eyes still fixed on her face. The grandmother stiffened and held her breath. She watched the dog's deep brown pupils. The girl didn't move her knees.

A minute passed. Then two minutes. The grandmother fancied that the dog's eyes were sad. She wanted to look at the girl's face, but she feared she might break the spell. Then the girl's right hand moved from her left forearm until it lay on her thigh. Her fingers crept slowly onto the dog's head. The delicate fingers rubbed the soft hair between the dog's ears. The dog whined softly.

The girl sniffed. Round wet stains appeared on the breast of her coat. The tears brought the grandmother's own tears welling and she fumbled for a tissue in her bag.

As her home station approached, the grandmother grew tense. She didn't want to part the girl from the dog, but she knew she wouldn't be able to stay sitting when the train stopped at her station. They could be hours waiting for another train to take them back.

'Our stop is just here,' she whispered to the girl. 'Time to say goodbye to Prince.'

The train ground to a halt and she stood up. 'Come on, alannah. Maybe we'll see him again.' She caught the child's sleeve and tugged it gently, but the girl pulled back. Her wet eyes pleaded as she stood up, but the grandmother looked away.

Walking up the road from the station, the grandmother searched for words that might ease the loss of the dog in the girl's mind. 'Isn't that man lucky to have such a lovely dog? He couldn't do without him, you know.' The girl ignored her. The woman felt the moment slipping away. They should have stayed on the train. Even if it meant staying the night in Dundalk, she should have left the girl with the dog. 'Ah, God help us all!' she said aloud.

The girl didn't eat her supper. At bed-time the grandmother sat on the bed side and began to read *Spikey the Young Hedgehog* aloud but when the girl turned her face towards the wall, she stopped. She hurried from the room because she knew she was going to cry. In the kitchen, she sat into the rocking chair and let her tears flow. It made no sense. Nothing had any meaning. The chair creaked as she rocked.

There was a movement near the door. The girl was standing there. The grandmother wiped her eyes with her sleeve, not wanting her tears to be seen. The girl came slowly to the rocking chair. The grandmother continued to rock. The girl put her hand on the woman's arm. She began to climb onto her lap. The woman reached for her and gathered her in. The girl pressed herself against the grandmother's breast and drew her knees up to her chest. The grandmother's tears overflowed but she turned her head so that they wouldn't splash on the girl's hair.

When many minutes of rocking had passed, the girl lifted her head and looked up at the grandmother's face.

'Granny,' she whispered, 'Can we get a dog?'

Joe Buckley was born and raised in East Offaly. He graduated as a teacher from UCD in 1967 and taught mainly English in a variety of schools in Canada and Ireland before finishing his career as Head of English in Salesian College, Celbridge. Joe and his wife Marion live in Maynooth and they have three sons and two grand-daughters. A keen sportsman, Joe also plays fiddle with Push for Porter. He has had five novels for young adults published. This is his first published short story.

The Strangeness He Had Felt All Day

By Tony McGettigan, Dundrum, Dublin

His annual visit to the grave of his parents evokes a lot of memories and reflections on how his life had turned out since Timothy had walked away from his first love all those years ago. He felt strangely different than for many of his previous visits.

TIMOTHY'S ANNUAL VISIT to his parents' grave usually evoked only a cold sense of duty fulfilled but today, today he felt, well, strange. He couldn't put it any other way. Strange, that was it and it surprised him. He tried to understand why but couldn't grasp it, couldn't get it clear in his head.

The cemetery was on the side of a tree-tufted hill overlooking the small town where he had been born. A few flower-laden graves that seemed to challenge death were intermingled with old unkempt ones that appeared to have grown comfortable with it.

Timothy turned from his parents' grave and looked down on the town. He had spent the unfolding years of his life there, the formative ones as they say. 'I'm in the unravelling ones now', he thought.

His family was not from the town, they were 'blow-ins'. There was no one local to maintain the grave so Timothy drove down from the city once a year to make sure that it was neat and clean. His visits had never been more than a rushed, get-it-over-with routine, an obligation. To whom or to what he wasn't sure, yet he felt the obligation and carried it out robotically once a year. But this year was different.

He had felt strange from the start, even before he left the city. It had been raining heavily and he was more reluctant than usual to make the trip. When he was getting into the car, he stepped into a puddle leaving his feet wet and cold. As soon as he was on the road, he turned on the heater and directed the heat down to warm his feet and dry his shoes. They had dried unevenly, one wrinkled and grey, the other wrinkled and black, as if from different pairs.

The sound of the rain and the swish of the wiper blades had made him lonesome. Something tightened around his heart, squeezing it empty. He felt an irretrievable loss that he had not felt before. He could not pin it down, could not clarify it, not even to himself. It irritated him and he said out loud, 'What the hell am I doing driving two hundred miles. For what? It means nothing to anyone. The dead don't care and neither do the living.'

Then he felt bad about that and tried not to think about it. He pushed on the radio. All the pre-selected stations had earnest discussions or noisy pop music. His tension increased. He tried using 'station select' but kept hitting the wrong button. He looked down to find the correct one and veered towards an oncoming car that flashed its headlights and sounded its horn aggressively. He gave up and stabbed the radio off. The strange feeling persisted. Maybe it was just a sudden awareness of his own mortality, of life slipping away, of things longed for that had never been achieved, and never would be now; things lost that could not be recovered or, worse still, thrown away never to be retrieved.

He broke his train of thought and concentrated on the town and valley below the hillside cemetery. He had experienced great loss there; the loss of his parents, the loss of his love, yes, the loss of his only love. It had been his own doing, deliberately. Of course, he was young then and did not understand. Yet, he could not excuse himself for it, had never excused himself for it on the many occasions he had thought about it during the long years since then.

When he had left the town at nineteen, he had left Joan behind, knowing the pain he was causing her. With the callous optimism of youth, he thought her love easily replaceable. It had never been. How sad, he thought, that at the age at which we feel most intensely, we value least what we feel.

He tried to break his uneasiness by examining the cemetery around him more closely. The crowded headstones bore many a familiar name. Making his way among them, he had stepped over, or passed by, the graves of several friends and acquaintances of his youth, of thirty five years ago now. Yes, it was thirty five years since he had left to go adventuring.

Was he sorry now that he had gone, that he had not taken the job that would have allowed him to stay and be with Joan? Why had he not returned to, nor even kept in touch, with the girl whose hand in his had thrilled him? Even the simple touch of her hand had thrilled him. Had he really felt like that, experienced that pleasure? Had he once been capable of such richness? Had that been him? Even his cynical distrust of sentiment, developed and nurtured over the years, did not allow him to deny it.

He looked away again over the town. The rain had stopped. A low, autumn sun flickered through broken cloud, scattering golden light over the valley. Somewhere a robin called repeatedly before bursting into song. There was a smell of earth and vegetation. The air was clear and fresh. Things stood out sharply. The cool of the dying year settled on his flesh.

The town was a grey stain on the green valley. A black river divided it. A fragile looking bridge tried to hold the two parts of the town together. The black river – could it be mere water? It looked like polished metal. Small boats were stuck on it. The soft, moist valley was enclosed by low hills, some kept in place by blankets of trees, others by ropes of straggling hedgerows.

The entire scene throbbed with the sweetness and mystery of life. When growing up, he had explored the woods and hills and fields around the town with the same excitement and wonder as that of the great explorers he liked to read about. But he had turned his back on it all and lost it. It no longer inspired wonder and excitement, only memories.

Examining the scene below, it seemed to him that nothing had changed much. The grey stain of the town had spread a little, maybe, but that was all. He tried to pick out the street where Joan lived, Joan Quirke, the girl he had loved and left behind. His heart had beaten faster every time he passed her door.

She couldn't still be living there, could she? In that street, in that house with the bottle-green door in the shallow alcove, where they had talked for hours, close together, reluctant to part? He had never felt that way again, after he had made the break, after he had gone adventuring.

He thought he could pick out, among the hills on the far side of the valley, the spot where he had kissed her for the first time, where they had kissed for the first time. They were sheltering from a summer shower, under a great chestnut tree. The birds had ceased their singing. There was no wind. It was very quiet. The steady fall of gentle rain was the only sound.

The canopy of chestnut leaves had begun to drip. Large drops sparkled at the tips of the broad leaves before tumbling to the grassy floor. One fell on Joan's upturned face. He kissed it away. Then they kissed for the first time, their lips wet and soft with rain. The memory squeezed his heart till he thought it stopped.

He sighed, turned back to the headstone on his parents' grave and read the simple inscription for the umpteenth time, his father's name and date of death, 'and his beloved wife', his mother's name and date of death, 'sadly missed by family and friends' and, at the bottom, just above the gravel coverlet, 'May their sweet souls rest in God'.

A brief inscription that hid rather than commemorated their lives. It said nothing about them, their love for each other and their children, their hopes and achievements, disappointments and victories. Feeling their loss, he wiped tears from his eyes with the back of his hand. The child, not the man, grieves his parents. Great monuments are raised to much less worthy people.

But his parents would not have wanted anything more than their simple headstone. That was part of their greatness. Yet their lives were not much different to those of the others all around them in that cemetery; unique lives, in a whole so great that individual uniqueness is easily overlooked.

How did his life fit into that whole? What contribution had he made? How had he affected anyone? Who would remember him with love and tears?

Suddenly, the strangeness he had felt all day became clear to him. He understood it but he put it out of his mind quickly. To distract himself, he turned again to the headstone and re-read absentmindedly its simple statement.

Space had been left at the bottom of the headstone for the names of any of their children who might wish to be buried with them. But none had. The oldest of the family, Philip, had died in England and was buried there. His English wife and children wanted it that way. Pat had died in Australia. His sister was still alive and married with a family in America.

And he, the youngest, after many years in different cities in different countries, had returned to live and work in Ireland. He was thinking a prayer for all of them, living and dead, when he was startled by a voice close behind him.

'Excuse me. Sorry! Are you one of the O Ryans?'

He turned around quickly.

'Oh, I'm sorry; I hope I didn't startle you.'

A pleasant looking, middle-aged woman was smiling apologetically at him.

'Sorry for interrupting your thoughts,' she said. 'I come here regularly, to visit my husband's grave. It's over there.' She made a vague gesture towards the other side of the cemetery.

'I knew the O Ryans well at one time, very well, so I usually pay a quick visit here too. I never saw anyone at the grave before. I hope you'll pardon my curiosity. When I saw you here, I wondered if you were one of the family. I lost touch a long time ago, many, many years ago now, but I knew them well.'

'Yes. I'm one of the O Ryans. Thanks for visiting the grave.'

'I knew the family well, in the old days; you must be Philip.' He did not correct her. 'I'm Joan Quirke, who was.'

Suddenly the years fell away and he recognised in the middle-aged woman before him the beautiful young girl he had loved and left behind. She offered him her hand and, when he took it in his and shook it, he felt happy and confused.

'I'm really pleased we met, Philip. Do you remember me? It's been a long time. What a coincidence! I'm on my way home. I'd love to hear all about the O Ryans. Would you like to stop in for a cup of tea and a chat before you head away? I'd love to catch up. Where are you living now?'

'Thanks, I'd love that too,' he said. 'Thanks very much. I'd love to. I drove down today.' She turned to walk to the exit gate. He fell in beside her, already comfortable in her presence.

'By the way Joan, I'm not Philip; I'm Timothy, Tim O Ryan, do you remember?'

She stopped and turned and looked steadily into his eyes for what seemed a long time. But she said nothing. He saw surprise and, he thought, gentleness in her eyes. He touched her arm to re-start their walk towards the gate and his heart beat faster.

Tony McGettigan has had five books published by Woodpark Publications, Dublin. Three are hard-back books co-authored with photographer Francis Twomey – Beara: The Unexplored Peninsula; Lovely Flows the Lee *and* The Inhabited Islands of West Cork. *He was writer and photographer for* The Ascent of Mount Elgon, *an account of a real-life personal travel adventure, and he wrote* The Letter, *a love story set in Kerry and Dublin. He has three times won prizes in the* Ireland's Own Open Short Story Competition. *He is a widower living in Dublin and his interests include writing and reading, hill-walking, theatre and music.*

My Mother's Blue Chair

BY MARY CONLIFFE,
ROBERTSTOWN, CO. KILDARE

The backless blue chair, discarded by the travellers and rescued from a briary ditch, was my mother's favourite bit of furniture, which she put to many uses …

A N OLD WOODEN blue chair with no back was my mother's practical working piece of furniture in our home in Borris-in-Ossory. Where did the chair come from in the first place? The story goes that one day my sister Teresa and I were out walking with our mother in the country when suddenly she announced to us: 'Do you see that broken chair in the ditch surrounded by briars? I wonder could you both get up on the bank and hand it out to me?'

The chair had been abandoned by the travelling people who had used it to sit by the fire in the evenings talking in little groups, or while sitting on it to make silver coloured tin tool boxes and buckets. The travellers in their horse-drawn colourful barrel-top wooden caravans visited our area every year, moving into a lay-by beside Coffey's farm.

Their advent brought a freshness into our lives and we always made them welcome. We children remained curious as to their lifestyles of which we were slightly jealous.

'Can you not get the broken chair yourself?' we answered our mother.

'Watch me,' she said and jumped into the deep, briared bracken, scraping and scratching herself in the process, her speckled cross-over apron getting tangled up in the briars as she tugged on the chair legs. We then jumped in to help her and out came the chair after our joint frantic pulls.

'I will find many good uses for this wooden chair,' she said, delighted with her new find in the ditch. This was a most exciting adventure for me to be involved in. My mother carried the chair home in triumph. She then scrubbed her new acquisition and painted it turquoise blue.

The chair's flat, almost square, top ensured complete safety when standing on it to perform tasks inside and outside the house. 'Where is my blue chair?' mother would shout out to us. She was known to run frantically from room to room looking to see where she last had left her famous chair. Did she use it to change an electric light bulb or did she climb on the chair to see into her kitchen dresser where she had left the car keys?

My mother had a lovely, carved, white painted wooden shrine with statues of the Virgin Mary, Saint Jude and Saint Teresa high up in the corner of her bedroom. Here she frequently hid little items under the precious statues, including her favourite piece of jewellery, a gold chain from aunt Anne Cleere, which she had received after her trip to Detroit in 1974.

Holy water bottles from the Cistercian monastery in Roscrea, along with other relics, were stored in this little space. Mother produced them if someone was sick or doing an important exam or was otherwise in need of divine assistance.

I remember one day she came back from a short stay in hospital and the first thing she did was to fetch the little blue chair in order to stand up and look into the depths of the shrine to see if her gold chain was still in its secret position.

The chair was also used to stand on when tuning the radio on its high shelf, and to find items such as candles, matches, letters, mice poison and other little treasures on top of the kitchen dresser. No other chair would do; it had to be the blue flat chair. Summer time saw it used as a stand to paint and clean the windows and doors.

I can remember having to climb on it to help find a chicken hatching out her chicks high up in a turf shed.

When in January 2010 my mother Kitty passed away, I brought her chair from Doon farm to my home and gave it a fresh coat of blue paint. I find it so handy for climbing when painting and cleaning my windows in my own home in Robertstown, and I think of my mother and her little eccentric habits when doing my tasks.

My only grandchild, Isabella Conliffe aged four years, stands on it and helps me make bread, cakes, jams and apple tarts along with playing at the kitchen sink. She also uses it to play with her tea set in our garden where we all enjoy a cup of tea served from the famous blue chair which Isabella turns nicely into a small little table.

The golden rule is to never cast away a broken chair with no back; it can be an unappreciated treasure.

Mary Conliffe, nee Cummins, was born in Borris-in-Ossory, Co. Laois, and has lived in Robertstown, Co. Kildare, since 1978 with husband Kevin. They have a son and daughter. She became an air hostess with Aer Lingus in 1971. She graduated with a B.A in 2006 and a H.Dip in History in 2007 and she holds a Masters in Local History. Mary has had a number of short stories published and contributes to Ireland's Own.

What Annie Would Have Wanted

By Liam Donnelly,
Stewartstown, Belfast

McClaverty wasn't especially good with kids, but he was available and was often called upon for the school run and the occasional 'night out'. He is minding five-year-old grandson, Aodhan, and finding the going quite challenging …

McCLAVERTY was fresh out of ideas. He had exhausted his repertoire of amusing stories, animal impressions and sleight-of-hand tricks. The five-year-old boy was unimpressed. He sat motionless on the couch opposite McClaverty. He hadn't uttered a word throughout the whole performance. He just sat there, his piercing blue eyes intelligent and quizzical.

McClaverty frowned and scratched his head. A lock of grey hair broke ranks and dangled between two bushy eyebrows. He combed it back with his fingers and grunted. The boy cracked a smile. He seemed to sense McClaverty's frustration. 'Smart kid', thought McClaverty, 'they warned me about that'.

McClaverty wasn't especially good with kids but he was available and lived close to his married children. He was often called upon for the school run and the occasional 'night out'. Since he lost Annie he had to be Granda and Granny. It's what Annie would have wanted. His gaze fell on Aodhan.

'You're not going to give me any trouble, are you?'

Aodhan shook his head. 'No, Granda.'

'Good boy.'

McClaverty looked out the window and sighed. It was still raining. Time moved slower on a rainy day, sometimes it stopped altogether. He remembered those long grey days of childhood, trapped behind misted over windows tracing pictures on the cold panes with his finger. There was no television in those days.

Now, there's a thought. He stared at the dormant wide screen television and the array of black boxes on the shelves beneath, each with its own umbilical cord, each with its own remote control. He studied the neat row of little black coffins and wondered out loud.

'Which one of these things turns on the TV?'

Aodhan didn't answer. He swept past McClaverty and pressed a hidden button somewhere along the bottom of the screen.

'You're dopey, Granda.'

'I know,' said McClaverty as he retreated to the comfort of an armchair. It was going to be a long day. He fluffed up the cushions and stretched out as the television stirred into life. Aodhan had the remote control. McClaverty didn't mind. If it kept the boy entertained he would put up with it.

Something annoying was clawing and clutching at McClaverty. He woke with a jolt. Aodhan was tugging on the sleeve of his cardigan. 'What?' he said, a little louder than he intended.

'You're snoring Granda. I can't hear the TV.'

McClaverty straightened in his seat and looked at the clock. It was 2.40 p.m.

'Thirty minutes. What was I thinking, falling asleep and leaving a five-year-old child unattended all that time?' He shuddered when he thought of all the bad things that might have happened but thankfully, hadn't. He roused himself and stretched. He needed a stimulant.

'I think I'll get myself a coffee,' he said to no one in particular.

Aodhan wheeled round from the TV. 'Can I have some juice, Granda?'

'You may have some juice.' But the grammar was lost on the five-year-old.

'And can I have some biscuits too?'

McClaverty smiled. 'Follow me'. He made for the kitchen but Aodhan got there before him. He switched on the kettle. Meanwhile Aodhan had lifted a bottle of orange juice from the fridge and was wrestling with the cap.

'Here, let me help,' said McClaverty.

'No, Granda. I can do it myself'.

Independent, resourceful or just wilful, McClaverty couldn't decide. The coffee tasted good. He prised the lid off the biscuit tin and rummaged through it. He settled for some digestive biscuits. Aodhan watched with rapt attention as McClaverty buttered and sandwiched them.

'Can I have one of those, Granda?'

McClaverty studied the array of chocolate goodies on offer in the tin and brought it eye level with Aodhan. 'Are you sure you don't want one of these?'

'Actually, I'd rather have one of yours.'

McClaverty smiled as he buttered more biscuits. Barely five and using words like 'actually'. He doubted if the boy actually knew the meaning of the word. He concluded that the child was a born mimic with a good ear for words. Both his parents were teachers and that would account for his advanced vocabulary. He piled the coffee, the biscuits and Aodhan's juice onto a tray and they trooped back to the living room.

Aodhan wedged himself beside McClaverty in the tight confines of the armchair. McClaverty found it uncomfortable yet comforting, invoking memories of his own small children. Aodhan munched his biscuits.

'I love these, Granda.' Biscuit crumbs lined his mouth and littered his lap. McClaverty smiled and sipped his coffee. He was warming to the boy. 'Granny used to butter my biscuits.'

Aodhan's thoughts carried him to a far place.

'What was Granny like?'

'She was beautiful. Just like your Mammy.'

'Had she black hair like Mammy?'

'Black as night. And lovely blue eyes – just like yours.'

McClaverty was spirited away to his own far place. He no longer heard the soft murmur of the television or the whisper of the rain on the windowpanes. Aodhan broke the spell.

'I'm done, Granda,' he said, wiping his mouth with his cuff.

McClaverty drained his coffee mug and tried unsuccessfully to raise himself from the armchair. Aodhan laughed.

'We're stuck, Granda.'

'I know.'

'You're too fat, Granda.'

'You're too fat.'

'Big fat Granda,' he chuckled.

'Wee fat Aodhan.'

McClaverty made great theatre of getting out of the chair, grunting and groaning as he prised himself free. Holding his hip, he hobbled to the kitchen with the dishes. Aodhan cracked up.

McClaverty settled back in his armchair. Aodhan went back to the TV. After a fruitless search through the channels he sighed, 'Granda, I'm bored.'

'What do you mean, you're bored?'

'I'm bored. I want to do something else.'

'Okay. What would you like to do?'

'Can we play a game? Daddy plays games with me.'

McClaverty was mildly concerned. He had no head for computer games and he wasn't up for anything too physical. 'What would you like to play?'

'I'll show you.' He took McClaverty by the hand and led him to a large cardboard box of toys underneath the staircase in the hallway. Aodhan rummaged through it and came up with a Star Wars Light Sabre. He frowned. They would need two for a proper fight. Something caught McClaverty's eye.

'Is that a baseball bat?'

'Yes Granda. Will you show me how to play baseball? Please Granda, please.'

McClaverty handled the bat with all the assurance of a novice. He knew all there was to know about hurling but nothing at all about baseball. He had played 'rounders' as a boy. That was similar. Perhaps he could bluff his way.

'Wasn't there a ball that came with this?'

Aodhan plunged into the box and surfaced with the ball. McClaverty hefted it in his right hand. He wondered why Americans called it 'softball'. It was hard as rocks. He considered the picture window in the living room and the wide screen television and tossed the ball back in the box.

'We can't play with that in the house. It's too dangerous.'

'Ach, Granda.'

'We can go out to the back garden when the rain stops.'

'But I want to play now, Granda.' His lower lip quivered and tears were not far off. McClaverty winced. He ran his fingers through his hair and pondered. At last he said 'I know what we'll do. We'll practice our swings with the bat. What do you say?'

'That's a good idea,' said Aodhan, a smile breaching the clouds.

'And when the rain's over, we'll go out the back garden and play baseball. What do you think?'

'Brilliant, Granda.'

Back in the living room McClaverty struck a pose with the bat. It was based on images he had gleaned from old movies and American sports on TV. The bluff worked, Aodhan was impressed. McClaverty was impressed. He demonstrated slow motion swings and explained how you should never take your eye off the ball as it was pitched at you and how, at the right moment, you should smack it with all your might. Aodhan was bouncing with excitement.

'Let me try, let me try.'

McClaverty passed the bat to him and rested a steadying hand on his shoulder.

'Now, hold the bat tight and look straight ahead.' Aodhan shuffled around for comfort and poise. 'The pitcher is out there right in front. Don't take your eyes off him. He's pitching the ball. It's coming right at you. Get ready, here it comes.'

Aodhan tensed as the adrenalin surged.

'Now, WHACK that ball right out of the park.'

There were two things that McClaverty couldn't have known. One, Aodhan was a southpaw. Two, he was standing on the wrong side of him. Aodhan's swing was mighty. It knocked the imaginary ball right out of the imaginary park and impacted on McClaverty's shin bones with a sickening crack.

There was a split second of silence before the pain receptors kicked in. The searing pain was exquisite. A primal shriek unleashed a four-lettered and ugly expletive. He wrapped his arms around his wounded shins and writhed on the floor. Once over the initial shock he worried that he had frightened the child.

He needn't have worried. Aodhan was rolling around the floor too, clutching himself but it wasn't from fright or fear, just the opposite. It was rollicking laughter, the kind that brings tears. McClaverty soon forgot his pain as he listened to Aodhan. The boy was parroting the expletive over and over again. McClaverty was horrified.

'No, Aodhan. You mustn't say that. It's a bad word.'

But Aodhan just laughed and swore, his diction clear, precise and unmistakeable. McClaverty seized him by the shoulders and he stopped laughing.

'You must never, ever, say that word again.'

The child's face darkened and McClaverty loosened his grip.

'Promise me you'll never say that word again.'

'I promise Granda.'

'Good boy.' McClaverty patted him on the head and limped off to the kitchen in search of some strong painkillers. He tried to put the whole episode out of his mind but it kept coming back to haunt him over the weekend.

Monday morning came and the word was out. It spread like measles through the P1 class. The principal of Our Lady Queen of Peace sent for Aodhan's parents. They were mortified beyond words. To be called before their boss to explain how and where their child had picked up such language was the ultimate embarrassment. Siobhan knew the source and so did her husband John. Her father would have some explaining to do.

When the phone call came, McClaverty wasn't surprised. He was half expecting it. Siobhan related to him the embarrassing interview with the principal. Although there was no finger pointing, the conversation was cool and terse. He hadn't been accused so he could offer no defence. But he was the culprit. Everyone knew it but no one said so.

It left a sour taste with McClaverty. He felt hard done by. No one would know the mitigating circumstances of his fall from grace. He wondered if anyone really cared. He got angry. He was always there in a crisis, unpaid and unacknowledged. What would they do if he wasn't there? He had all day Tuesday to think about it. He was in turmoil. None of his children could afford to fall out with him. His services, flawed as they were, came free. Child minder fees were eye-wateringly expensive.

He felt used and exploited. 'To hell with them,' he thought, 'Let them row their own boat.' But then something started gnawing away at the back of his mind. It was Annie. Not her words but her wisdom, a soothing balm to quell his anger and assuage his pride. On Wednesday morning he would be there to mind Aodhan as usual with his usual smile. There would be no words of recrimination. That's what Annie would have wanted; always his sage – gentle, loving Annie.

Liam Donnelly in 1990 worked up the courage to join Conway Mill Writers group on the Falls Road in Belfast. In a lucky break, his very first story was taken up by Pam Brighton (R.I.P.), a BBC producer who was visiting the group to give a talk. She took it home and had it broadcast on BBC 4 six months later. She produced two more of his stories in the early 1990s and another story was broadcast on Radio Ulster. He is still with the Conway Mill Writers, now in the role of facilitator. He has also had three stories published in Ireland's Own, *one in the 2012 anthology.*

The Last Summer

BY HILARY DALY CASTINE,
PARKER, COLORADO, USA

*A little girl living in London spends her summer holidays with
her grandparents in rural Ireland and is left with happy memories
that will last a lifetime, especially the adventures and tall tales
shared with Pop, her granddad …*

MY GRANDFATHER NEVER liked goodbyes;
he said he'd already said too many in his lifetime.
So every year on the last morning of my summer
holiday, he'd hug me so tight I thought my ribs would crack
then head out into the strawberry field without a word. There
were no long, drawn-out farewells, no tear-stained goodbyes.

But one year that just wasn't enough for me. So when our
cases were loaded into my uncle's car, I ran through to the gap
in the hedge eager for a proper goodbye.

'Pop, pop, we're leaving, I …' But before I could finish, he
waved me back.

'Don't come any closer. I'm spraying the strawberry plants;
it'll make you sick,' he said, adjusting the sprayer on his back.

I stopped, tears brimming my eyes and whispered, 'Goodbye Pop.'

He lifted the cap from his head in salute. 'Go on now,' he
said. 'You'll miss the ferry.'

Had I known that that summer, my seventh summer, would be
his last, that I'd never see him again, I would have run to him,

ignoring the sprayer, disregarding the ferry and I would have hugged him. But children don't think about death. They don't think about cancer stealing tomorrow. They only think about now, and I was no different.

It had been an idyllic summer. 1970, the first summer of a new decade, the kind of summer Hollywood makes sentimental movies about. It had started with an early morning taxi ride to Paddington Station, a rare treat for our working class family. Then on to Fishguard via a long train ride, shortened by colouring books, card games and salmon sandwiches.

But the most exciting part of the journey was the ferry across the Irish Sea to Rosslare and the adventure it promised. Stormy or calm, I didn't care. I had made the crossing every year since I was born and had great sea legs. The rougher the sea, the more fun I thought it was. Even when most passengers were hanging over the deck depositing their breakfast in the churning sea, my family could be found devouring fish and chips in the restaurant.

We were always careful to save a handful of chips for the seagulls that followed the wake of the ship. The sight of the gulls skilfully snatching up chips with their beaks before flapping away, pursued by their greedy cohorts, thrilled me.

When the chips were gone, and the seagulls had lost interest in us, we'd head to the front of the ferry eager for the first glimpse of land, and of Pop waving from the pier. Anticipation bubbled in my stomach as a long summer with my beloved grandfather stretched out before me. I wasn't his only granddaughter, but he made me feel like I was when I was with him.

Pop was known for being a bit of a character; a kind-hearted soul who knew no strangers and would give you the shoes off his feet, but would also spin you a tall tale just for the craic.

I was the victim of one such tall tale when Pop enlisted my help on a run to the local shop. I balanced precariously on the back of his rickety old bicycle as we bumped down the dirt road. He weaved from one side of the road to the other, lifting his legs in the air, pretending we were flying; I held on tight to him, equal parts delighted and terrified.

The visit to the shop was as much a social call as it was about buying the butter we'd been sent for. I sat in a corner savouring the ice cream. Mr. Stamp, the shop owner, gave me as a welcome back gift as the old friends discussed the goings on in the area. 'The church roof is leaking again,' began Mr. Stamp. 'There'll be a second collection on Sunday to pay for repairs.'

'Best leave straight after communion then,' joked my grandfather.

You'd think the two men hadn't seen each other in months. They talked about everything from where the fishing was good, to the state of the world beyond. But Mr. Stamp left the best piece of gossip for last.

'Did you hear Murphy's bull got out again? Caused quite a ruckus in the village,' he grinned.

I sat up, full of attention; this sounded like it was going to be good.

'Knocked Mrs. Kehoe's garden gate down and trampled her prize geraniums,' he continued.

'Prize geraniums?' questioned my grandfather.

'They weren't officially "prize" geraniums yet, but according to Mrs. Kehoe they were guaranteed to win first prize on Saturday at the flower show,' said Mr. Stamp with a chuckle. Then, standing to attention, his nose stuck in the air, he changed his voice to the nasal tone of Mrs. Kehoe, "until that great brute of a bull trampled them out of existence".'

Both Pop and I started to laugh at his impersonation.

Mr. Stamp, obviously enjoying the attention, leaned over the counter. 'I heard she was so upset that both the bull and Mr. Murphy were in mortal danger. It was divine intervention that Father Doyle was on the scene to chase her down and remove the garden rake from her hand.'

At that my grandfather doubled over with laughter and I knew full well I'd hear the story again but coming from Pop's lips the bull would be bigger and Mrs. Kehoe even madder.

The real mischief, however, did not occur until the ride home. Pop rode past Mr. Murphy's cabbage field, but then slowed and circled back, stopping at the gate. He signalled me to hop off the bike. Glancing furtively around, he stashed the bike in the hedge. Pop pressed his index finger to his lips, turned on his heel and tiptoed into the field, raising his knees in an exaggerated manner. He looked like a cartoon character.

I tried to stifle a giggle, but to no avail. I snorted loudly. Pop froze in his tracks. He looked around again, turned to me pressing his finger to his lips again and shushed me. When he was sure the coast was clear, he resumed his cartoon walk into the field. Not knowing what was going on, I shrugged and followed, tiptoeing in the same exaggerated fashion. Pop searched the rows of cabbages as if for treasure.

'Not that one; maybe that one. No, too big, no too small.'

Up and down the field he went.

'Not green enough, too green.'

The sun started burning the top of my head as I watched him, my arms folded across my chest. I was about to call out to him when he clapped his hands.

'Aha, the perfect cabbage,' he announced before disappearing behind the leafy cabbage plant.

'Don't tell Nanny,' he whispered as he shoved the cabbage into my arms. 'We'll eat well tonight,' he said.

We jumped back on the bike and sped off like two bank robbers with their loot. I'd never been involved in such a caper before; I couldn't look in my grandmother's eye when I handed her the cabbage. I didn't find out until later that Pop had an arrangement with the farmer: potatoes in return for cabbages.

Now it wasn't all play during the summer, no indeed, I had to earn my keep or more accurately, my sweet money. My grandparents ran a modest farm, just a handful of acres where they kept chickens and a few pigs, but their primary income came from the strawberries they grew for the jam factory. It not only helped my grandparents, but it was also a wage earner for the whole community.

Members of our family and neighbours came from miles around to harvest the berries. Adults were earning extra money to help feed their families or buy something special, chilren saving for schoolbooks. For the adults it was backbreaking work, bending down over the fruit laden strawberry plants for hours on end.

For us children, being closer to the ground was an advantage. We'd scoot up and down the drills on our bums or knees, our clothes growing heavy with soil. But no matter how old or young you were you had to obey the rules of the field or risk being chastised by the other pickers. Once you started a drill, you had to pick every ripe strawberry on that drill before you moved on. There was no drill hopping, no matter how big and succulent the strawberries looked in another row.

Your earnings were calculated by the weight of your bucket at the end of the day. Truth be told, if I had put more strawberries into my bucket than into my belly I would have earned a lot more money. But how could a child be expected to resist a perfectly ripe strawberry with a smell so sweet it sets your mouth to watering the moment the scent reaches your nose. I barely had time to rub the soil off them before they were in my mouth.

Up and down the drills we'd go, stopping only for the Angelus, and to drink tea and eat jam sandwiches at lunchtime. As I worked, I listened to the adults spinning yarns. I joined in when the field broke out into song. And I'd dodge over-ripened strawberries hurled at me by my older cousins.

When the midges began circling our heads and nipping at our ears, Pop would ring a bell to signal that picking was over for the day. Young and old, we'd all stand up in the drills, moaning, stretching, clutching our backs, and complaining about our weary bones. We'd struggle to the top of the field with our heavy buckets, daydreaming about the coins that would soon be jingling in our pockets.

Pop always made me his helper, which made me feel important. He'd load the strawberries onto the weighing scales, and I'd read the numbers. My favourite task was putting the hard-earned money into the strawberry stained hands of my fellow pickers. The top picker always got a little bonus. I dreamed it would be me one day, but my strawberry stuffed belly predicted otherwise.

When all debts were settled, the crates of strawberries stowed safely away, and the pickers gone home to their suppers, we'd return to the cottage for our own. A hard day's work done, I'd barely get through my meal before sleep claimed me, the smell of strawberries lingering on my hands.

When we weren't working in the strawberries, my grandfather took me through the lush green fields, pointing out foxes and birds and teaching me the names of trees and crops. In the evenings, I'd sit at his feet staring into the open fire as he told me stories of his younger days.

That is how he passed the last summer of his life. Not having fabulous adventures in distant lands, but by creating memories for a little girl to cherish.

Even now, when many decades have passed, and I have said too many goodbyes myself, the sweet smell of strawberries transports me back to the last morning I shared with him. I can hear my seven-year-old self, standing in the gap in the hedge calling to him. I can see him look toward me one last time. I can see him lifting his cap in one final farewell.

This time, I do not whisper goodbye, I whisper 'Thank you'.

Hilary Daly Castine was born in London to Irish parents. They moved back to County Wexford in her late teens. She worked in retail in Enniscorthy, got married in nearby Monageer and is now living in Colorado, USA, with her American husband and two adult sons. She still has strong ties to her family in Wexford, to where she often returns. She has been a writer/producer in the television/cable marketing industry for more than twenty years. She learned the art of storytelling through her parents, Mary and Peter Daly, who filled her childhood with their stories.

Let There Be Light

By Maura Flynn,
Westport, Co. Mayo

*A revolution was wrought in rural Ireland in the 1940s and
'50s when 'The Power' was introduced into homes and businesses,
bringing light and the miracle of radio at the flick of a switch
to many people for the first time.*

FOR MONTHS WE watched the men, knee deep in water, digging holes for the ESB poles. Not every one agreed to let them dig on their land, and rows broke out over where the poles should be situated. Most people were suspicious about letting 'The Power', as they called it, into their homes.

Brigit, the priest's housekeeper, said she would not touch the light switch with her hand, so Father O'Malley came up with the bright idea for her to use the handle of the brush to turn the light on and off.

All our houses had to be wired before the big switch-on, and we watched with excitement as holes were drilled in walls and wires dangled from ceilings. Dust rose in clouds as walls were disturbed for the first time since our house was built years before.

Mam was busy sweeping all day, trying to keep the dust at bay, and she wondered if it would be worth it. But her sister, who was a nurse in England, advised her to have patience and put up with the dust, as she would not know herself when she had light at the flick of a switch and, best of all, the radio at the turn of a knob.

We never had a radio before, and the only time we heard one was in our Grandmother's house when the neighbours gathered to listen to the All-Ireland final.

Every day as we walked home from school we watched the ESB men hoist the giant poles into the sky; they changed the landscape completely, and even the cattle in the fields seemed to be fascinated by them, plus they made great scratching posts.

When all the poles were in place, the men started to string heavy wire from one to the next, like a giant necklace blowing in the wind. The wire came, wound around large timber wheels like the spools of thread Mam used when sewing.

How that was going to create light we had no idea. One joker in the village told us it would happen when lightning made contact with the wire, and as I hated lightning I began to look at this with a wary eye.

Soon all the field work was done and the poles stood proud and tall, waiting, like us, for the big day. A man from the radio shop went from door to door selling radios. My Mam settled on a Bush model, a marvel of polished wood and shiny knobs. It had the names of all the stations we could get behind a little window. At the turn of a knob you could move a marker back and forth to select the station you wanted to listen to.

A special shelf, with brackets underneath, was put up on our kitchen wall, out of the way of little fingers, and we were warned not to climb up and move the dial, as the radio shop man had fixed it at Athlone, all ready to spring into life when the switch-on happened.

Then the big day arrived and we could hardly conceal our excitement at the thought of what was about to happen. Oil lamps were filled for the last time and Mam scrubbed the house from top to bottom, because she said the new light would show up all the cobwebs in the corners; families of spiders that had lived there for years had to scurry for their lives as she wielded her feather duster.

A switch-on party for the adults was arranged for our local hall, and we stayed at home with our big brother in charge. We were warned once again not to touch anything as the switches were already on for the light and the radio.

Our parents got dressed up for the big occasion and, with a few final warnings to do as our brother told us, they set off for the local Pembroke hall for the big switch-on. We could hardly contain our excitement as we waited for light to appear, and better still, the radio to burst into song.

Then it happened! Suddenly our kitchen was filled with the brightest light we ever saw. But wait a minute, where was the music we had waited so long for. All we could hear was a solemn voice in a language we did not understand coming from our radio high up on our kitchen wall.

Someone's little fingers had moved the dial and instead of getting Athlone our radio was tuned in to Vatican City. So we spent the night listening to Italian voices coming over the wires to our house in the west of Ireland, as we were afraid to touch the dial in case we broke the radio.

Maura Flynn lives in Westport, Co. Mayo, voted the best place in Ireland to live. She and husband John have four adult children. She has been retired for six years. She belongs to a writers group called Ward9writers that published an anthology in 2012. Another anthology is in the pipeline. She has been published in Ireland's Own *over the years.*

The Games We Play

By Pauline Clooney,
Newbridge, Co. Kildare

The celebration of Christmas is portrayed as a great family occasion, a time when young and old join together for that special dinner, fun and games, but it can often be an occasion when tensions can come bubbling to the surface …

THE GRANDMOTHER wore a purple, paper crown that was held in place with ladybird clips borrowed from the youngest grandchild. Every so often she patted it as if to check that it was still in place. The others had lost theirs earlier on in the evening or had taken them off.

She held her fanned cards close to her chest, tilting her head down over the double chins to look at them.

There were accusations earlier about 'reneging' and 'not robbing', all ending when The Mother cleared the table with the same sweeping movement used to clean it with the dishcloth. As tears pooled the Mother's eyes, she had apologised. She said she was tired. She said there was a lot involved in getting the Christmas dinner and she always worried about little things like the amount of onion in the stuffing or maybe a power cut. She said the ESB weren't beyond throwing the kibosh on the festivities with their strikes.

The Child seemed happy to see them playing cards again as she smiled at her mother and gave her father a thumbs up. Every so often the Father would interject with reassuring platitudes.

'That turkey was lovely and moist, Mother, you have the knack, alright, basted to perfection.'

It was hard to read the Grandmother's face. Was she agreeing with him? The Mother stared at her each time but the Grandmother gave nothing away.

'Did you enjoy your dinner, Grandmother, you're saying nothing?' The Mother said.

'I'm half afraid to voice an opinion after your previous little strop,' she said.

'I think it's time for a cuppa and a bit of Christmas cake, what do you say to that, Maw?' The Father looked anxiously at The Mother. He called her Maw when he was being affection-ate; playful. It was short for her name.

The Mother's movements in the kitchen were snappy, deliberate, her arms conducting. The gush of water filling the kettle stilled her momentarily as if she was witnessing something she had never seen before. The white icing on the cake seemed resistant to the serrated edge of the knife and The Mother leaned forward and over it, pushing down until it glided through the packed fruit. She cut large, generous slices.

Still wearing the mantle of peace broker, The Father offered his annual festive philosophy,

'Well, it's as far away now as it ever was,' he said.

Throughout the adult shenanigans The Child continued playing Ludo with her sisters. The Grandmother had brought the children a compendium box of games. The cover of the box promised hours of fun for all the family but they only recognised two games in it – Ludo, and Snakes and Ladders. They couldn't play Snakes and Ladders, the youngest was afraid of snakes, so Ludo it was.

121

At the start of the evening they sat upright, expectant, but those poses had slipped and slouched, so that they now reclined at awkward angles on the couch, empty chocolate wrappers and half-eaten bars strewn around them.

Santy had brought The Child and her older sister musical typewriters but they had been assigned hours earlier to the top shelf in the cupboard under the stairs. The racket had been too much for The Grandmother. The Child's typewriter was blue. Before it was confiscated she could play "Twinkle Twinkle Little Star" on it. When she accompanied the Pope that morning giving his *Urbi et Orbi* message on the television her father clapped and said Liberace wouldn't get a look in.

The Mother won the first game after the tea. As she drew in the pile of coins, The Grandmother's jawline began to set, her lips were pursed and she straightened her back, thrusting her ample chest forward.

'I'm parched; could someone get me a mineral?' she said.

'Child, get your granny a glass of lemonade,' The Mother said.

The Child had no sooner left the couch, in answer to her mother's request, when The Grandmother continued: 'I think it might have been the cake, it was fierce dry; you didn't put enough whiskey in it.' The statement was directed at The Mother.

The Father looked at The Mother, a combination of fear and pleading in his eyes. The Mother folded her arms and sat in her chair, her chin pointing up at the paper decorations draping from the ceiling. She made a sort of kissing sound with her lips before she spoke.

'It took a lot of eaten cake for you to figure than one out.'

She followed up with angry words about greed; about whose

recipe was being used in the first place; about compliments always sticking in certain peoples' throats.

The youngest, the one with the snake phobia, started to cry and a guilty silence descended. Nobody noticed The Child placing the glass at The Grandmother's elbow.

With a determined, scooping movement, like a theatrical croupier, The Grandmother swept the stash of money into her cupped hand knocking over the drink. The lemonade spread like a breaking wave, soaking everything in its wake. The Grandmother, with angry red circles dotting her cheeks, announced that she wanted to go home. This was a new departure; she always stayed until the day after Stephen's Day.

The Child went back and sat with her sisters asking whose turn it was to throw the dice. The Father, rubbing his hands together, even though the house was warm, leaned his head in the direction of the Grandmother and whispered.

'Be the hokey, maybe there was too much whiskey in the cake after all,' he said.

The Grandmother whipped her head away and shot him back a dirty look.

The Mother got up and went to the scullery to get the dishcloth. As she passed the cut cake on the counter she pinched up a few crumbs and chewed them slowly with knowing nods of her head.

Lifting cups and then cards in one hand and mopping with the other, The Mother announced: 'Sure, you can't spend Christmas night on your own, it wouldn't be right, The Child will go with you, so.'

At the mention of her name The Child threw a startled look, first to The Mother and then to The Father. The Grandmother didn't miss a beat:

'Right so, you better give Mick a ring.'

Mick was her son and the only one in the extended family to have a car. The Father voiced his concern that Mick would have a few drinks in him, because of the day that was in it. But The Mother, in encouraging, enthusiastic tones, said he'd be grand, with no other cars on the road there would be no fear of him.

Nobody seemed to notice The Child. She widened her eyes as big as she could, slightly tilting her head back, as she gulped down the lump in her throat. The Father winked at her. She didn't give him a thumbs up this time.

The Grandmother waited for her son in a chair by the kitchen door, her coat was buttoned to the collar, her scarf tied firmly under her chin, her black bag, clutched with both hands, was perched on her lap. The Father turned up the television. The Mother cleared off the table. The Child went upstairs to pack a bag and cry openly.

Mick sang Jingle Bells on a loop between the two houses. The Father had been right earlier about the drink, however all obstacles were avoided and he waited in the car until his mother and niece were safely through the front door and the hall light turned on. Two beeps of the horn and he screeched the car around, speeding back down the road.

The house was cold and there was a stench of stale urine in the hallway. The Child's nose twitched. She left her bag at the end of the stairs and went into the kitchen. She turned on the television and sat at the table, folding her arms and resting her chin on them, watching the black and white picture taking shape.

The Grandmother was a flurry of activity. She hauled a gas heater over from its perch beside her armchair by the range and she placed it beside The Child. While standing with one finger pressed on the ignition button as the red glow spread through the grid, she stretched over to the window and pulled the curtains with the other hand. In the back kitchen she put on a saucepan of milk.

When The Grandmother placed the mug of cocoa on the table, The Child, without looking up, said she didn't like cocoa anymore. The Grandmother disappeared into the front room and came back with a heavily taped cardboard box. With exaggerated gestures, as if it was a speed test, she opened the box and emptied out the contents. A variety of Rowntree Mackintosh products spilled on to the table. Her youngest daughter living in England worked there.

She invited The Child to take whatever and as much as she wanted, she said they could have their own secret Christmas feast.

The Child refused, she said she was sick of chocolate. The Grandmother scanned the room anxiously, like one frantically looking for something they'd lost and when her eyes fixed on the dresser she suggested that The Child should get a chair and bring down the deck of cards from the top shelf and she would teach her how to play twenty-fives.

'Wouldn't it be gas if next year you just sat at the table, maryah, and told your daddy to deal you a hand?' she said, 'I'll teach you about robbing and reneging too, that's where the real fun is.'

In an uncharacteristic outburst The Child straightened up and told the old woman exactly what she thought of her cocoa and her sweets and her cards. She cruelly reminded her of the bucket of 'wee' upstairs that she had forgotten to empty and she said all she wanted to do was go home to the Christmas decorations and play with the musical typewriter that she got from Santy.

The Grandmother looked taken aback at the outburst as she straightened up, thrusting her chest forward. She hissed at The Child. 'Ah, there's no such thing as Santy, you're auld enough now to know that.'

The Child was silent.

The Grandmother was also silent as she slowly put the sweets back into the box and stuck the masking tape back along the join of the lid, all without glancing at her granddaughter. She left it in the middle of the table and plopped down into her armchair by the unlit range, joining her hands on her lap as she circled her thumbs.

The National Anthem was playing.

The Child reached over and reopened the box, taking out a Yorkie. She carefully unwrapped the bar as if it was a Christmas present, and pointing the exposed chunks at the range said:

'Granny, I think you need to get rid of that and build a proper fireplace…with a chimney.'

The Grandmother nodded and said she would.

A white line travelled in a continuous motion down the television screen, as the last strains of Amhrán na bhFiann faded away.

Pauline Clooney is a native of Portlaoise. She teaches English, history and creative writing at the Patrician secondary school in Newbridge, Kildare. She holds an M.Litt from NUI Maynooth (2006), and an MA in Creative Writing from UCD (2015). She is working on her debut novel. She is the founding director of the Kildare Writing Centre. She won the RTÉ Guide/Penguin Ireland Short Story competition *and was placed second in the Doolin Short Story competition (both 2015).*

The Wake

By Patricia Carr,
Fanad, Co. Donegal

I murmured a quiet Rosary and reflected that this might well be the only religious aspect of this young lad's Irish burial. There were no tombstones on the sea and no markings in 'Calvary', the make-shift graveyard in which 'washed in' bodies were interred …

THE TRANQUILITY OF the setting was in stark contrast to my reason for being here. I tried to put the unpleasant aspect of the night watch to the back of my mind. My heart bled for his family. Their fine son taken in this crazy conflict, his body washed up so far from home. This could be my own uncle, killed and buried in Burma, unknown to those who dug his grave.

I gently lifted the sheet covering his face. I touched his joined hands. They felt clammy and cold. I was not afraid. He looked like a gentle soul and tales of ghosts and ghouls never bothered me anyway. It was going to be a long night. I decided to take a break and left the hut for a while.

The wind, like the croak of an old raven, at first caressed the moonlit Atlantic swell. A growing storm rose around my ear-drums. It whipped the calm sea into a frenzy. Every seventh wave smashed itself to pieces against the rocks and cast its arms skywards. The thunder of the white horses' hooves could be heard across the bay. They were at full gallop, driven by the Northern storm.

I rolled my uniform trench coat tightly around me and stood awhile to watch this unfolding drama. A freak wave propelled itself onto the promontory on which I stood. I gasped and swallowed a mouthful of the effervescent froth as I staggered in the path of the blinding spray. The briny taste soldered itself to the roof of my mouth. A second wave threw itself over me and thundered into the air. A feeling of disorientation gripped me and I realised that I should get back to shelter.

Dripping wet, I hastened to the safety and comparative comfort of the ramshackle hut.

The winds buffeted the door that hung loosely on its hinges, but I managed to secure it without too much difficulty. I combed my hair with the wind of my hand, threw aside my soaking trench coat and sat down. I clapped my hands and rubbed them together in an effort to restore the lost feeling. The echo of this simple task startled me in the heart-pounding audible silence. Stretching myself on the makeshift settle bed, I felt the swirl of the gale as it lulled me into an uneasy sleep.

When I awoke it took me a minute to figure out where I was. What was that constant, nagging, dripping sound? In the hazy semi-darkness I realised that this was the water running off my oilskins onto the frigid slate of the floor. The steaming stench of my other clothes – like that of unwashed corduroy and wet wool drying out – lodged in the back of my throat.

In spite of having been lit for hours, the Stanley 8 range was still radiating warmth, and my first thought was to keep it stoked up. A puff of smoke ghosted out as I opened the fall-door to increase the draught. The heathery sods sparkled and sizzled as their sparks were drawn up the chimney and into the night sky. Soon, the old black kettle was puffing steam. The heat reached out for me. Its gurgling lent a slight homely air to this dark and dismal setting.

The tea was bitter and had a slight taste of mould. In the stillness, I could hear every mouthful as I slowly swallowed. Having put the cup back on the rickety shelf, my thoughts turned once again to my lifeless charge.

The match rasped as I struck it off the bottom of my toe-plated shoe. The candle light flickered sideways in the draught, almost dying out only to flare up again with renewed luminance. It cast an eerie sloping light over the corpse. Little patchy hillocks of shadow emphasised the general shape of the body underneath.

Death permeated my senses – the sight of this lifeless bundle, the lingering moulding scent in my nostrils which dripped into my throat, the covering sheet, rigid and icy to touch, and most bizarre of all, the haunting noise of the throat rattle as excess air was being expelled. He was somebody's son and this was his wake.

I murmured a quiet Rosary and reflected that this might well be the only religious aspect of this young lad's Irish burial. There were no tombstones on the sea and no markings in "Calvary" – the make-shift graveyard in which 'washed in' bodies were interred. I blessed myself as I finished my recitation. It was then I realised that the wind was lisping gently through the cracks in the door. In the hope that the storm had passed, I took a furtive look through the grime-smudged window.

On my second venture out, the scene was transformed. As if guided by the touch of an Almighty hand, calm had descended. The air had salt and the sweetness of seaweed on its breath. Rooted to the spot, I watched the spine-tingling sight of the round pale moon as it rolled into view from behind Murrin Hill. At first it looked like a giant Tilly mantle, too delicate to touch. Its growing light slotted into a dip behind the hill, making it resemble for a moment, a giant origami.

In next to no time the moon was out over the sea, leaving a trail of golden light on the water. The breeze played a tune on my ribs, a cold melody but one that was deliciously invigorating. The Atlantic swell had been transformed from frightening to serene with the rise and fall of the winds and tides. The potential power of these two natural elements taunted and thrilled my soul in equal measure.

The musical rhythm of the waves was like a voice on my shoulder. It whispered: 'remember me.' I was transported back to my Granny's knee. Smelling the salt-laden air and inhaling the wonder of my surroundings, the tale she told me as a child, sounded credible now:

'God created Ireland and his job was nearing an end. He found that He had an assortment of scraps left over. Waste was one thing that, above all else, He detested. "Let me see," He mused, "I could use these to fill the gap between Melmore and Malin." God's ragbag was upended and it spilled forth gems, the like of which was not seen before. After His Sunday rest, God set about putting these in order. The result was a rich mosaic of sea and sky, hill and glen, deep water lochs, wildlife wetlands and towering trees. He called this peninsula Fanad and placed it as the second highest point in the country.'

The intermittent gleam of the Lighthouse – man's contribution towards the magic of Fanad Head – cut across my childhood musings. Its swathe of light complemented the fading moon as it illuminated the darkening stretch of sea. I shielded my eyes as its brilliance swept landwards towards me before it faded in the huge globe. In the shadow of the darkness, I could just make out the answering flashes of Tory Island and Horn Head lighthouses towards the west. Malin Head's flare was ghosted against the horizon. Nearer hand, Dunree Head reflected in the Lake of Shadows – the Swilly – completed this symphony of sea, headlands and wordless beamed messages.

This was the darkest time, that brutal hour just before dawn. I gazed over the rim of the cliffs towards the sea. This sea, which had yielded up its dead in raging spates, was now tranquil, gently re-shaping the sleeping shingle as it ebbed and flowed. Was this symbolic of things to come? Would the hatred of these brutal times be consumed in waves of reconciliation? Would that I was able to beam a message to the unknown mother, sister or wife of the lifeless young man unceremoniously waked in a tumble down outhouse. I would tell them that he had been recovered and buried in 'Calvary' – hopefully one of the last, as we consign this ramshackle resting place and this terrible war to the annals of history.

Born in March, 1947, Patricia Carr is a native of Fanad, Co.Donegal. Her first foray into writing was in the early seventies when she was a founder member of The Fanad Magazine Committee. After her retirement as school secretary in 2007, Patricia took up writing again. A keen competitor in writing competitions, her entries were highly commended in Ireland's Own Anthology in 2013 – 2015 and again in 2017. Fluent in Irish, widely travelled and an avid reader, Patricia is single and lives with her faithful dog 'Misty' and five cats.

A Presidential Visit

BY MUIREANN MACGAFRAIDH,
ATHBOY, CO. MEATH

*Recalling the great excitement and euphoria that gripped Ireland in
1963 when John F. Kennedy made history by being the first sitting
President of the United States to pay an official visit, and my
Dad's small part in the massive occasion …*

IT WAS JUNE 1963 and Ireland was in a state of euphoria. President John F. Kennedy was on an official visit to
Ireland, the first ever sitting president of the United States
to set foot on Irish soil. People spoke about nothing else.

The first I heard about it was at school. The nuns informed
us about it and that we should be thankful to God for such
a wonderful visit and we were to mention our thanks in our
prayers and to especially pray for good weather.

For weeks before the visit we learned all things American,
such as how many stars there were on the American flag and
why. At choir practice Sister Kevin taught us 'The Battle
Hymn of the Republic' and 'If I Had a Hammer.' We entered
into the spirit of things and spoke Americaneeze; we thought
Americans spoke as in the cowboy films. We greeted each
other with 'Howdy folks, how's ye all doing?'

The Principal was not at all impressed when some younger
pupils responded to her 'Good morning girls' with 'Howdy
Sister.'

It got even better when we learnt that my father would be driving one of the state cars. My mother got into precision mode and decided that dad's black work coat and suit would have to be cleaned and pressed. Not the usual brush, iron and a wet sponge method, but the meticulousness of the dry cleaners. Mother was determined Dad would look the part.

The coat went directly from the dry-cleaners into the large wardrobe in the big back bedroom until the day of the President's arrival; until then Dad wore his second best suit and borrowed his brother's black overcoat.

Windows were washed. The net curtains were taken down and the best white laced ones went straight up. The footpath outside was scrubbed clean.

The day dawned, finally. Mother stood in the hall and inspected Dad before he set off for work. She eyed him from head to foot like a sergeant-major inspecting the troops before the big brass arrived.

She ensured his tie was straight, that he had his leather gloves, and his flask of tea and sandwiches wrapped in the greaseproof wrapper of a Johnson Mooney and O'Brien sliced batch loaf, packed into his lunchbox. Yes indeed, Dad had gone up in the world; mother had provided him with ham and cheese sandwiches no less. As Dad exited the hall door he was greeted by the neighbours who had gathered to wish him 'the best' and to shake his hand.

Over the next couple of days we barely glimpsed my father. The radio was on all day long. We had television, but back then television had limited hours. Radio still ruled the waves and it was filled with Presidential news. We heard Kennedy's address to the houses of the Oireachtas and presentation of the flag of the Fighting 69th Irish Brigade that fought in the American

Civil War. We learned that the sword of Robert Emmet sat on the Presidential desk.

On the last day of The Presidential Visit dad drove a brilliant ebony and chrome car home and parked it outside the hall door. The car was immense and palatial. We pestered him so much that he finally allowed us five minutes in the car.

We were overawed that President Kennedy had sat in the very place we now occupied. We sat encompassed in the luxuriousness of leather seats with arm rests and spotless ashtrays. The car smelled of leather, wax polish and pungent aftershave. It had the heady unfamiliar but totally appropriate odour of poshness.

I realise now, of course, that it was not the presidential car. Back then my father told us about Kennedy, 'that he was a sound man with a grand smile and teeth as white as piano keys.' My father was a teller of tall tales and funny stories and we hung onto his every word. Soon our time was up and we were whooshed out, back to reality and the hardness of the footpath, bicycles and shanks mare.

I browsed through old photographs recently and came across an old black and white photo. It has three men top to toe in black, stood inclined against a long sleek ebony car, my father is in the middle; each man conscious of the sense of occasion but with broad smiles. It's dated June 1963.

My Mother and my Aunt were in the Fairview Cinema in November 1963 when word went about that President Kennedy had been assassinated. My father died four years later. I never got to ask him about Kennedy's Visit and who had sat in that glorious car.

In their fashion both men had the gift of the gab and the articulation of dreams. When the world was easily amazed and charmed, and dreams really could come true.

Muireann MacGafraidh was born and raised in Dublin, and has a grown-up family. She lives in a small village in rural county Meath. She worked abroad for some years. She now works part-time as a Home Care Assistant (HCA).

The Flowers of Glengarriff

By Joseph Sweeney,
Blarney, Co. Cork

*There, by an old railings flaking with rust, he found a headstone
covered in moss and lichens. He lowered his head and looked at the
grave. He wasn't sure why he had come, exactly, or what he was
expecting before he saw this overgrown unmarked grave,
the embodiment of neglect. He felt a secret ache that had
been within him since childhood.*

SEAN FLEW INTO Shannon just before noon on a spring
day in 1982. After coffee in the airport cafeteria, he drove
south in a hired car, grabbed some lunch in Cork city,
then headed west. Through purple mountains haunted by late
afternoon shadows, through the Pass of Keimaneigh, Béal na
Bláth and Kealkill he drove, on to the crossroads at Ballylickey
bridge, and the final run into Glengarriff.

He signed in at reception in the Eccles Hotel, went up to his
room and, after standing and staring out over Bantry Bay for a
moment, he lay down on the bed and closed his eyes. Dislocated
memories of childhood began to arrive, like curious birds, but
as he stumbled towards them, to check if they were real or
imaginary, they flew off, one by one, and he fell asleep.

It was evening when he awoke, got up, showered, dressed
and went down to the lobby. The eyes of the girl at reception
followed him as he made his way across the lobby, a dark-
haired young man in a tuxedo, with a bright red carnation

in his buttonhole, with a shoulder bag. He caught her eye as he approached the revolving doors. Today was Valentine's Day. He smiled at her. The guys back in the New Jersey office had been amused when they discovered that Sean's birthday was February 14th. Fancy having your birthday on Valentine's! You're a born romantic, Crowley.

As he emerged from the hotel a brusque spring wind was blowing. The sea was agitated, a slow dark swell accumulating against the land. On the horizon the sun was a great red ball.

With the thumb of his right hand hooked under the strap of his shoulder bag, Seán made his way through the village. A gust of wind tossed his long brown hair back as he passed the old stone church. Smells of fish, salt and seaweed hit his nostrils, and something else he couldn't pin down, something he remembered from childhood, some indefinable wild smell of the sea. When he came to the orphanage he placed his shoulder-bag on the low wall. There was a clinking sound from a bottle of Moet and Chandon, and two champagne flutes inside.

Sister Imelda smiled the moment he walked in the door, as if a day had not gone by since he had left.

'It isn't! Seán Crowley?' She took both his hands in hers, then stood back and surveyed him.

Later, stirring the tea pot in the reception room, she said there were crocuses by the bed the day he was born. 'White, they were, your mother's favourite spring flower.'

She went silent, arranged her napkin unnecessarily.

'I remember the birth,' she said, nodding. 'She fought for you, with her last breath, tugging at God's clenched fist, opening it, finger by finger, until He released you, out of His great and mysterious palm.' Sister Imelda's eyes were shining. 'You were like a mussel. Not moving. All scrunched up. We thought you were dead … too.'

The old nun lowered her eyes and stared down at the table, and receded into a world peopled by ghosts, nuns in white habits, passing each other in corridors, brass crucifixes settled on their chests.

'Alphonsus thrust you under a cold tap. You gave a little shudder, clenched your fists, your pudgy cheeks drew back, and you screeched as we wiped the blood away.' She paused. 'It was a little miracle. Just as your mother died you drew breath.' She lowered her shining eyes. 'She looked so peaceful in the end. She got just one glimpse of you, and then she died with a smile on her face.'

Sister Imelda poured some more tea, nudged the plate of scones towards him, and questioned him about his life and work in New York. As he was leaving he asked what his mother's real name was, and where she was buried. She told him, and described where the grave was.

A girl in a pink coat was walking down the street as he made his way to the graveyard. About the same age as his mother, he thought, according to Sister Imelda, only fifteen. His mother was never more than a school girl, a school girl with a world of dreams that had all died with him.

The young girl met his glance and smiled. He imagined his mother smiling. He watched her disappear into the garden of a little cottage.

He sat on the low graveyard wall, with his back to the Caha mountains, facing out towards Bantry Bay, westwards across the Atlantic, towards America, the old New World, the great escape. Tomorrow he would be back in New York, Ireland just a memory again.

The air tingled with the rawness of spring. He placed both palms on the wall, felt the stones. Perhaps his mother had sat here once, back to the mountains, dreaming of a new life. Maybe she'd sat with his father, whoever he was, the two of them holding hands; or maybe she sat here, on the cold wall, alone and pregnant, worried, not knowing what lay ahead. Maybe it was just he and his mother, the same living thing, on this wall, closer to each other than they could ever be again.

The young girl, cradling an untidy bunch of flowers, waved goodbye to an old woman in the doorway of the cottage, and made for the graveyard. Seán stood up as she passed him, put the strap of his bag over his shoulder, went through the narrow iron gate, followed the path as it wound around the dead. He passed the girl standing at a grave, clutching the white flowers, caught a scent in the wind as she stooped and laid them out on the white gravel. Crocuses!

Outside the low wall, down a cobbled lane, flowerless hanging baskets creaked on their chains. Two young mothers pushed their prams idly forwards and backwards, talking as they did. Occasionally they stooped to tuck a blanket tighter, asking their babies questions. Rising and falling in the wind, their sing-song voices straggled over to him. He heard a baby giggling in delight. The young mother straightened, her face alight.

After a long search he found the corner Sister Imelda had directed him to. There, by an old railings flaking with rust, he found a headstone covered in moss and lichens. The putt-putt-putt of a fishing trawler chugging into the bay came to his ears. He watched as it nudged its way slowly back into the harbour in the gathering dusk. As the boat grew closer with a broken halo of seagulls above it, he could hear the hungry screeches. He watched the distant white bodies dragged back and forth, tireless in the gusting winds, desperate to feed themselves and their young.

He lowered his head and looked at the grave. He wasn't sure why he had come, exactly, or what he was expecting before he saw this overgrown unmarked grave, the embodiment of neglect. He felt a secret ache that had been within him since childhood.

He looked up at the darkening sky. The wind rose with sudden energy, buffeted him and drove him from the grave, as if questioning what he was doing here, telling him he didn't belong here.

He recalled Sister Imelda's parting words to him, as she had walked with him down the convent avenue. Our lives are brief in the context of eternity. Love is our greatest achievement, and love sometimes means sacrifice.

A robin descended on the headstone. The wild rambling rose leaned in the wind, its naked, thorny stems trembling. Small buds, like tight baby fists, shook from side to side.

'Gather ye rosebuds while ye may.'

Some evening, he thought, when he was reading in Central Park, maybe with a mug of coffee and a doughnut beside him on the bench, these buds would open and a gentler breeze come and sprinkle rose petals over her grave.

Pop! Phsssshe!

Pink bubbles burst up in a gushing fountain and streamed down the outside of the Champagne bottle. He poured until both flutes were brimming, leaned over and placed one in front of the head stone. At first he had thought it was blank but now, close up, he noticed something carved into the stone. Stooping closer, he pulled away some moss and made out a date. February 14th, 1956 – his birth date, written in stone, the date that would unite the two of them forever.

He raised his glass, and then took out a piece of paper on which he had written some words that he had planned to read over her grave. A powerful gust caught him unawares and he tightened his fingers instinctively around it. He clenched his fingers around the paper for a moment then lifted his hand, opened them, and let the wind snatch the paper from his hand.

Tears streamed down his face, unseen by anyone. He was one of life's castaways, a shipwrecked passenger, snatched from the uncertain sea, taken from his mother by the same wave that dragged her out and under; washed to shore in the same tide, the same breath. They would never meet, never see each others faces, not even for an instant again, perhaps not for all of eternity. A love that never had a chance. Unless, one day, resurrected, they sailed into some great Heavenly bay together, in another better life, a country where they would both be welcome, where love alone would bind.

The wind grew stronger. Trees and hedges shook and the graveyard seemed to come alive. The two young mothers with the prams shrieked, as a sudden violent gust threatened to snatch their prams away from them. They clung on, laughed and shielded their babies from the sea wind with their bodies. The crocuses that the young girl had gathered were whipped up from the grave and into the air. She ran after them, earnestly, as they flew off like birds. Each time she caught up with one and stooped to retrieve it, the wind lifted it again out of her reach.

Down the cobbled lane the hanging baskets were swinging wildly back and forth in the wind. The trees shook madly, as if trying to uproot themselves. Sean knelt and kissed the headstone on his mother's grave. For a moment it seemed like he was the only thing in the world not moving and then his grip was broken by the power of the wind. He gasped, stood up and turned his back to the sea.

A moment later the wind died down and he turned back to the grave. The Champagne glass had blown over. It lay there, empty but unbroken, pillowed on thick green moss, the champagne gone, as if she had drunk it. He stooped, took the glass, filled it again until the sparkling pink liquid frothed over the edge, and placed it in front of the headstone. He touched his own brimming glass against his mother's one, then took the red Valentine carnation from his button hole, and laid it upon the gravestone.

As he left the graveyard a feeling of unexpected peace came over him. He had come home … to himself, to the truth. To where he had begun.

When he got back to the hotel the receptionist smiled. He approached the desk.

'Happy Valentines!' she said. 'I see you lost your carnation.'

'Happy Valentines!' he said, taking out the half finished bottle. 'How about some Champagne?'

She laughed. 'I'd love to but I can't, not while I'm working.'

'That's alright,' he said. 'Maybe later?'

'I'd like that,' she said.

'Great! What time do you finish?'

Joseph Sweeney was born in Dublin and graduated from UCD with an honours Master's Degree in Anglo Irish Literature in 1983. He was a teacher of English and French until becoming a full time writer in 2007. Novelist, short story writer and humorist, he has been the recipient of the Bryan MacMahon Short Story Award, a first prize in the Cross National Short Story Competition, and now two first prizes for humorous essays at Listowel Writers' Week. His work has been broadcast on RTÉ radio, including an appearance on Sunday Miscellany. He is the author of a collection of humorous stories and essays entitled Tilting at Windmills *[Amazon.com].*

Freedom

By Tina Sweeney,
Enniscorthy, Co. Wexford

*A group of Enniscorthy rebels came out in support of the 1916
Easter Rising and briefly took control of the town before it became
the last place in Ireland to surrender. These true events provide the
backdrop to a story of true love as old as time itself …*

SUNLIGHT CREEPS CAUTIOUSLY over the roof-
tops as I shiver in the early morning chill. From my
third-storey perch I watch the long shadows gradually retreat from the Market Square below as the strengthening
sun advances. The tall buildings huddle together around the
Square as their owners huddle together inside, feeding on
whispers.

The silent empty streets belie the tension that lurks behind
boarded up doors and windows. Though it is Sunday, Mam
says we will not go to Mass today, Father has forbidden it.
We have not left the house since the rebels took over the town
last Thursday morning.

I wonder if Father has returned with news. He was still
out when Mam sent us off to bed last night. We have hardly
seen him since Fr. Fitzhenry pressed him into service on the
Peace Committee. We are starved for news, like the rest of
Enniscorthy. Rumour and speculation abound; whispers pass
from house to house as if they have no need of carriers.

We hear there is a new Republic; then that Pearse has surrendered in Dublin. A neighbour tells how Fr. Murphy blessed the rebels, yet Fr. Fitzhenry negotiates surrender. No one knows whether to celebrate or lament. The town holds its breath as we wait for certainty to come. Many are coming forward to join the Volunteers. Some, like Father, try to limit the damage, fearful of British retribution.

'You're up early.'

I jump at the sound of my little sister's voice. She turns over in bed and I see a younger version of myself. Her dark curls are tumbled on the pillow and her merry green eyes twinkle with the eager expectation of a twelve-year-old child. The four years between us have moulded me into prim and proper Miss Roche, my skirts lengthened, my long hair pinned up, my green eyes demurely lowered before the men in my father's pub. Despite the seriousness of the hour, I cannot help but smile at the reminder of how carefree life used to be.

'Are you watching for the Volunteers?' Bessie grins. 'Michael can't be in every patrol, you know.'

I snatch a pillow from my bed and hurl it at her.

'Bessie, hush for goodness sake! Mam might hear you.'

'Oh don't worry,' she mocks. 'Mammy is so concerned about Father's safety she can't hear anything!'

'I wonder if Father is back yet.' I change the subject.

Bessie thinks my feelings for Michael are a joke, a useful barb to employ in sisterly rivalry. She is oblivious to the fire that could be sparked by her teasing if Mam should hear.

'I'm sure he is back,' she replies. 'Father would never stay out all night. I don't see why he has to be on the Peace Committee at all. He's not part of the Town Council.'

'No, but he is a respected business owner,' I explain. 'He said it was his duty to help restore order to the town.'

144

'The town seems pretty orderly to me. There has been no looting, and no fighting that we have seen.'

'Wait until the British arrive,' I warn. 'Do you think there will be no reaction from the Crown just because the RIC ran back to their barracks? The rebels have taken over the Castle and the Athenaeum. They have closed all the pubs – including ours. They have blocked all roads leading into town. How long do you think the British will let that go on?'

I turn back to the window, frustrated now by her childish ignorance. I blink back hot tears as I consider how my world – once as safe and innocent as hers – is now tumbling down around me.

'Oh Michael, where are you?' I wonder silently.

As if my heart has summoned him, he appears. He rounds the corner into the Square with a group of Volunteers, and instantly my eyes pick him out. Though they all wear identical uniforms, he is head and shoulders above the rest. His fair hair is almost hidden by the cap as I look down from so high above them, but I would recognise the proud tilt of his head anywhere.

My heart beats so loudly I am afraid that Bessie will hear it. As the patrol crosses the street he is directly opposite me – if he looks up he will see me standing in the window in my nightgown. Careless of my modesty I step even closer to the window, willing him to look up. I am sure that if his deep blue eyes meet mine the fear inside me will melt away. I will know without a word between us the intentions of his heart.

But he does not look up. He is a soldier now. I watch the tops of their uniform caps as they march right underneath my window, past my father's pub, and on down the street. He didn't even look up. The tears fall as my hot breath makes patches on the window.

This was to be our time. Over the Easter weekend, while Mam was busy with church duties, and Father was busy in the pub, we were to make our escape. We had it all planned. On Easter Saturday night I waited at midnight under the Cotton Tree, beside the bridge. But Michael did not come. I waited for hours, huddled in the dark shadow of the tree, terrified of discovery. Eventually, I retreated home.

I was sure there would be word. Somehow he would get a message to me; an accident, an unforeseen delay, new arrangements. Now I fear no word will be coming. 'Mother Ireland' has called, and I am forgotten. I am beginning to wish I had not succumbed so easily to the passion in those blue eyes.

Once more I see movement in the street below, and step back instinctively as my Father's stout frame comes into view. Even from this distance I can see the weariness in his walk, his usually upright stature bent beneath the weight of his task.

'Father's coming, get up,' I urge Bessie, and we hurry to dress so we can go down and hear his news. I am just trying to brush Bessie's curls into some kind of order when Mam bustles into the room.

'Mammy, what's happening? What does Father say?'

Bessie's excited questions are ignored as Mam's anxious eyes meet mine.

'Go downstairs and get your breakfast, Bessie. I'll be down in a minute.'

'But…'

'Now!' snaps Mam. 'And go quietly. Your Father is resting for a while. He has been up all night.'

I am filled with foreboding as Mam closes the door behind Bessie and turns to me.

'What is it?' My throat is so dry I can hardly speak.

'Ellen, you must tell me the truth,' she begins quietly, her gaze so intense I cannot look away. 'Have you been meeting Michael Ryan again behind your Father's back?'

Fear does not allow confession. I deny it emphatically even as my conscience cringes at the hurt in her eyes.

'Ellen, you were seen,' she whispers. 'Two different people reported it to your father last night, and one of them was Fr. Fitzhenry.'

'I hate this town!' I cry out, enraged at the spies. 'Full of busybodies and gossips …'

A sharp slap across my face shocks me into silence. In all my life my mother has never raised a hand to me.

'You fool!' she hisses. 'Those people were trying to protect you. What was just a daughter's disobedience last week has now become rebellion against the Crown. The Rising is over, Ellen. They're all going to jail. And if it becomes known that you are associated with one of the rebels, you might go with them!'

I am undone. The slap, her words, my situation – it is all too much. I cover my face with my hands and weep. My sobs soften her into pity and I feel her arms come round me. I turn my face into her shoulder and howl. I wish I could turn back into the security of childhood obedience but my foolish rebellion has pulled down all that was secure and right with my world. Everything lies broken, and I cannot fix it.

'I love him, Mam,' I whisper into her shoulder. 'He is strong and noble and brave.'

'Ellen dear, he's not noble or brave. He has been bewitched by poems and songs and dreams. That's not brave. It's not real.'

'He has risked his life for Ireland!'

Her arms are gone from around me and I feel the coldness as she moves away.

'Your brothers are risking their lives for Ireland. They are spilling their blood on French soil to secure Home Rule for

Ireland. That is noble and brave. That is real. And how will they feel when they come home to find it was all for nothing, overturned by a few madmen with rifles taking over buildings and intimidating decent citizens?'

I watch the fight go out of her. 'That's if they come home at all.'

'Mam,' I plead as she opens the door. 'Is Father very angry?'

'He's furious, Ellen. With both of us! I trusted you to keep your promise not to see that boy again. Your father stopped you going to those Gaelic League meetings – did you think that was the limit of his power? He allowed me to plead leniency for you because I told him you could be trusted. Your treachery has impugned my honour as well as your own.'

'I'm sorry, Mam.'

'You will be when you see the full extent of his control. He's talking about sending you up the mountain to your Aunt Moll! That's if you manage to stay out of prison.'

'Are you that sure it's over? I saw Michael's patrol just a few minutes ago.'

'The Peace Committee brought a copy of Pearse's surrender order up from Wexford this morning. But the crowd here refused to accept it. Colonel French has sent two of them up to Dublin by motor to hear from Pearse in person, though why he didn't just shoot them I don't know!'

'Maybe only the leaders will be arrested,' I suggest desperately.

'Or maybe they will all hang! Ellen, you need to just forget about Michael Ryan and start worrying about yourself. You would do well to get down on your knees and pray that your name is kept out of it.'

My heart breaks as the door closes. I collapse onto the bed, my sobs muffled by the pillow. Oh Michael, what am

I going to do now? I wrap protective arms around my stomach. I think of Fr. Murphy blessing young men to kill and die. I wonder if he will so easily bless a foolish young girl to bring life? I think not.

I am deserted as Michael chases heroic freedom. Was the smaller freedom we dreamed of together not also worthy of pursuit? No freedom now for any of us.

Bitterness rises like bile in my throat as I realise that, in the birthing of great and noble dreams, many sweet and simple dreams must perish.

Tina Sweeney is a native of Enniscorthy, and had her first writing success way back in the 1980s, when she had several stories published in Woman's Way *magazine. This impressed her so much that she forgot all about it and went off to get married and raise a family. She now lives in Oylegate with her husband and two almost grown-up sons. In recent years she has remembered that she used to be a writer and has thrown her hat in the ring once again.*

Neighbours

By Vincent J. Doherty,
Burford Gardens, London

Fondly recalling his neighbours in long ago Tyrone whom his grandmother described 'as rough as a bag o' nails', but for all their rough and ready ways they always offered a welcome to anybody passing, including a wandering schoolboy like himself.

THE McGETTIGANS WERE our nearest neighbours. My grandmother said they were 'As rough as a bag o' nails', the kind of people who laid newspapers on their table instead of a tablecloth, 'and not even dacent newspapers at that.' She disapproved of English newspapers.

Sure enough, theirs wasn't the most refined of domestic establishments. One time, when they had a young servant girl working around the house, she was boiling some potatoes in a pot and, wanting to know whether they were ready or not, took the lid off and without looking put it down on the table.

As luck would have it she'd put it on top of a bar of soap which stuck to it. Again without looking, she put the lid back on the pot. Talk about hubble bubble! The poor girl was distraught when she realised what she'd done but Barney, the man of the house and not one to waste anything said, 'Give them spuds to me. I'll eat them. Sure clean meat never fattened a pig.'

But for all their rough and ready ways they always offered

a welcome to anybody passing, day or night, including a wandering schoolboy like myself.

By the time I knew them, Barney and Ellen were getting on in years and always seemed smoky to me, the smell of a reeking turf fire in their hair, their clothes and even, I imagined, in the wrinkles of their weather-beaten skin. This mingled with the smoke from Barney's 'Sweet Aftons' and Ellen's clay pipe tobacco. And if it wasn't smoke, it was soot that sometimes blew down the chimney on windy days.

Even the tea canister sitting on the mantelpiece between two bored looking Delph dogs looked soaked with soot. Every so often the soot in their chimney would catch fire, sending sparks flying in all directions, threatening to set their thatch alight and giving us all an hour or two of harmless drama.

You couldn't call their house comfortable by the standards of today but it was cosy enough in its own way; flagstoned, it was badly lit and sparsely furnished with a table, a press, a few chairs and a picture of the Sacred Heart.

The old couple spent most of their days in front of the fire, often enough with their feet among the ashes in a huge hearth with a crook swinging to and fro. There always seemed to be food and drink on the go, Aran Banner potatoes from an ancient iron pot and Killybegs herrings in an equally ancient frying pan, with a jug of buttermilk to wash them down, and if not buttermilk, the kind of sweet tea you could stand a spoon up in. And every Wednesday there was the warm comforting smell of baking soda bread.

Theirs was a great house for ceilidhing (gathering together) which might go on till all hours, especially during those times of the year when nobody had to rise with the cock's crow.

Neighbours dropping in would get as near to the fire as they could, hear the latest craic and tell, retell and listen to the old stories about everything and everybody from Half-hanged McNaghten to Oliver Cromwell, from 'The Wild Man of Borneo' to Red Hugh O'Neill, adapted and added to as they were passed on by word of mouth and often relocated to the townlands thereabouts.

'I'll tell yous about the time of the Plantations', Barney would begin a tale of blood and thunder and the way he told those stories they might have been happening across the fields last month or last year. I never thought there was much interesting about Barney who seemed a quiet peaceful old man, until one of our other neighbours told me about his time in Derry jail.

He was in there doing seven days for something connected with poaching or poteen or some other nonsense but the day he was due to be let out he knocked one of the warders flat and got a further fourteen days hard labour, breaking stones on bread and water. He went up in my estimation after that.

I often dropped in on my way home from school for a cup of tea and a soda scone with raisins in it. Immodestly proud of my meagre educational skills, I would ask them, 'Would you like me to read to you?'

'You're a wee scholar,' Ellen would tell me. 'What does it say in Old Moore's Almanac?' The 'Almanac' was the only 'book' in the house, full of important anniversaries, birthdays, predictions and dates of fairs and feast days.

Kitchens like the McGettigans are the kind of places you only see in museums now and people like Barney and Ellen have long gone to their reward but they're still with me when I remember those long ago days.

Vincent Doherty was born in rural Tyrone during the last months of the Second World War but has lived in London for more than fifty years. He has always kept in touch with his Irish roots. He has spent most of his working life in education, teaching and working with young people nationally and internationally on a range of projects. He worked with the BBC presenter Peter White on a series of radio programmes called 'Children of the Olympic Bid' *about some of my young people who went to Singapore with the British delegation when London successfully bid for the 2012 Olympics.*

The Dream House

By Noelle Lambert,
Clonmel, Co. Tipperary

*After nearly seventy years Christopher has come back to Ireland,
and to the Big House as it was known in his youth when he
worked there as a gardener. It has become a hotel and his
granddaughter is having her wedding there. So many memories
come flooding back – times were so different then …*

S LOWLY HE MADE his way along the narrow path.
The aromatic bed was in full bloom and scents of
rosemary and lemon verbena rose to meet him. Amazing
that so much was the same. Had time stood still? Images from
the previous few hours crowded his mind; the country church,
soprano notes soaring through the timbered ceiling, Aveen,
his granddaughter, so beautiful in her gown of cream. Mrs.
Thornton-Walshe.

Strange how life played these games, he thought. It seemed
only a few months since Aveen had first spoken about her plans
to visit Ireland. A gap-year she called it. How had it changed
to this? To a bride, to a new mistress of the Big House?

That was what everyone used to call it – the Big House. He
had spent four years working on these grounds, yet today was
the first time he stepped through the front door. Welcome to
Knocklucas House Hotel he read on the brass plaque. Aveen
had embraced him, holding him tightly. Her eyes held tears
that glistened like dew.

154

The path curved; how quickly one was out of sight. The sounds of the wedding party dulled and he felt quite alone. Would it still be there? For some changes had been made, that much was clear. The stables were gone and the servants' kitchen.

Why feel sad for the loss of buildings, he chided himself, when the people were gone too. Passed away most likely. He had been one of the younger ones. The others were probably all dead.

Sadness was his companion then when he came on the house. It was there, still there, the Dream House. His eyes scoured the lattice windows, the thatched roof. Benches had been fitted between rose beds along the wall. He walked to the front door. A notice informed visitors that the craft shop and tea-room would be closed for the weekend to facilitate a family wedding. There was a menu too, in a glass case. The Dream House it read on top.

Leaning his right hand against the wall, he braced himself. It hurt to breathe; he must not collapse, he must not ruin Aveen's day. He straightened himself and staggered to the first timber bench. That was better. It had been a big meal, he just needed to rest. All the memories were hard to take. Memories…

'Excuse me,' she had called. 'Could you help me, please?'

That was what surprised him, the politeness of it, and she in pain, and she the daughter of Master and Mrs. Thornton. The housemaids spoke to him with less respect.

Her ankle was swollen. He offered to go for help but she shook her head, her eyes looking directly into his, unsettling him.

'I'd prefer not to be alone', she had said quietly. That was the way with her, she would not ask you straight out.

155

So he helped her to straighten up, then edged his way towards her horse. Taking the reins he brought the mare back to her.

'Poor Misty. You've hurt your leg too!'

She decided to move immediately then. He had to wrap his arm around her and help her hobble back through the fields. She chatted easily, explaining the accident, the pain in her leg, the wait, the relief when she saw him.

What's your name? she asked.

'Christopher,' he told her. 'Christopher Doyle; named after my grandfather and the saint of journeys.'

'I'm Sarah.'

Sarah. Like ripe plums clustered on a branch.

They rested occasionally, stopped for quite a while once when he found a tree stump for her to sit on. He took a bundle from his pocket. It was his mother's bread, still warm and wrapped in a checked tea towel.

'This is delicious,' she declared. 'What's it called?'

'Spotted dog!'

She laughed until she threatened to topple off the stump. 'That's the best name I've ever heard' she managed to say before she laughed again. He joined in. That was another thing about her. She made the day look full of joy and hope and fun.

And when the big house came into view, she leaned over and kissed him on the cheek.

'Thank you. Ask your mother for the recipe for me. I'll meet you at the old lodge this time next Sunday.'

The days passed slowly. He felt the length of every day, watching the house as he hoed the borders or put out the dahlias, recalling her every word, remembering the sound her laugher made in her throat. He hoped to catch sight of her when he was sent to prune the roses near the stables. He worried about her then. Maybe her leg was badly injured?

But there was nothing wrong with her leg when he arrived at the lodge on Sunday. She ran to greet him, smiling, a little breathless.

'I missed you so much,' she cried. 'I used to wake in the night longing to see you.'

He could not reply to such a declaration. 'I brought you more bread,' he said at last. 'And the recipe.'

'What's it called again?'

When he would not answer she smiled, stretched towards him and kissed him. On the lips this time. He wrapped his arms around her and every waiting moment was forgotten.

They fell in love during stolen moments at the lodge. In the safety of the old kitchen they curled up on a little sofa and imagined a future together.

'Our children will eat spotted dog for breakfast,' she would declare. Or, 'Do you like walking on the mountains? We should explore every mountain path in the Comeraghs. We could bring the dogs with us. We'll spend our lives enjoying simple pleasures.'

Once he tried to remind her of reality, their reality. 'The cottage I grew up in is smaller than this room,' he said.

But she raised a finger to his lips. 'This is our dream house. If we dream hard enough we can make our dreams come true.'

He held her and learned to dream. Outside, the world continued on its busy way; the first president of Ireland was inaugurated, traffic lights were installed in Dublin, Paddy, the head gardener, fretted about a German man called Hitler.

Inside, he grew to know the various expressions of her face, the softness of the underside of her arms, the way she giggled when he kissed her ear, the way she stilled when he drew his lips back from the base of her neck.

'I don't want you to stop,' she said. 'I don't want to be apart from you.'

But he did stop. He remembered his mother's tears when his sister Gertie started a baby, her chances of marriage ruined. He would not harm Sarah.

'I love you, Christopher,' she said.

'I love you too, Sarah.'

The end, when it arrived, was as unexpected as the first frost.

Paddy knelt beside him while they planted narcissi bulbs. Planting in August suited the bulbs, Paddy claimed, suited their temperament and allowed them to grow in their own time.

Christopher made a non-committal sound. He was wondering how he would survive the weeks when Sarah returned to school.

'Like, there's a place that suits everything,' Paddy said. 'And as you know, if you plant a shrub in the wrong soil or in the wrong spot, it will not grow.'

'Um.'

'And once certain plants are established, it is a great wrong to move them.'

'Uh uh.'

'I wanted to make sure you understood,' Paddy said, raising his wiry body and placing a mud covered hand on Christopher's arm. 'The harm that can be done to a beautiful plant if it is taken from its rightful place. You know that, don't you? Different soils for different plants.'

Christopher looked into the older man's face and saw that he had understood correctly.

'You're a good gardener,' Paddy said quietly. 'I can give you a recommendation.'

'Thank you.'

Christopher placed a bulb into the earth and covered it with soft, moist soil. She would walk past a sea of golden trumpets in the spring but he would be gone. His uncle in America had sent an invitation again last week. It was the only solution. He would have to tell her.

'Granddad, it's me. Are you awake?'

Startled, his eyes shot open. It was not Sarah. Not her blue eyes. He had woken too soon. There was something else he had to remember. He closed his eyes again.

'Please don't go,' she had pleaded. 'I'll beg Father. I'll beg Mother. I'll run away with you.' She had asked straight out, begged him.

'Are you all right, Granddad?'

He gazed into deep brown eyes, Aveen's eyes.

'Can't an old man shed a tear at his own granddaughter's wedding?'

'Ah Granddad! Is it lonely to see it all again? Sixty-eight years is such a long time. I hope you didn't mind Jack mentioning it in his speech. That you had worked here, I mean. Maybe you think that's private?'

'No need for all that privacy lark anymore. In my day you had a place in society and you had to stay there. I've lived to witness equality.'

'Well, Jack's father inherited the estate from his parents but it's hard work to keep it. That's why he turned it into a hotel. Jack and his brothers grew up with very little money. They've had to work hard for everything. I'm not expecting it to be easy.'

'You'll be great, Aveen,' he said, his voice a bit shaky to his ears. 'Take care of each other first and foremost.'

'Jack would love you to stay until we get back from our honeymoon. He wants to show you old photos of the family and staff. And I want you to stay so we can spend time with each other. The room is there for you and every morning after breakfast we can wander around the gardens and you can show me the places you worked. What do you think? You could just decide to live here indefinitely, your second retirement!'

'I could stay for a month or two,' he said slowly. 'Until August maybe. I'll plant narcissi for you so you can think of me in the spring. But the time will come for me to go home too. My burial place is on the other side of the Atlantic, with Eleanor.'

He expected her to tell him to hush, not to talk about these things on such a day. Instead she said. 'Of course, Granddad. It is good that I know your wishes.'

He nodded, satisfied. There would be no confusion. Here was his dream house, witness of his first passionate love. In Louisiana stood his home, witness of the life and family he had cherished.

'I must not keep you from your guests,' he remembered. 'Not to mention your husband!'

'Jack knows he's got competition,' she informed him. 'He knows it was my dream that you would travel over for our wedding.'

Ah, that word again.

Best not to expect happiness from dreams, he thought. But he did not say this. Maybe life would teach her different lessons.

She took his hand and helped him rise from the bench. Together they walked away from the Dream House, her young arm strong under his. They paused at the bend to take in the sight, Knocklucas House, resplendent as ever; people milling about on the lawns, laughter soaring, oak trees guarding the scene like sentries.

Sarah's grandson, Jack, came towards them. He carried her smile, that same flash of joy and hope. Aveen raised her free arm and waved but did not release her hold on him. He had never thought to wish for a loving arm to support him in his old age. The greatest gifts, he realised, might be those beyond our dreams.

And what is spoken remains in the room,
waiting for the future to hear it – T.S. Eliot

Noelle Lambert is a primary school teacher with a lifelong love of reading and writing. She is married to Joe and they have three young adult daughters. Noelle had two books for children published some years ago and has recently self-published a family saga set in Ireland ('Where Rowan Trees Grow', Amazon Kindle). She is delighted to share 'The Dream House' with readers as she believes a little romance and nostalgia are good for the heart and soul. Noelle lives and works in Clonmel, Co. Tipperary.

Picnic on the Island

By Mae Leonard,
Naas, Co. Kildare

Remembering a lovely sunny Sunday in 1948 when the whole family had a picnic on St. Thomas's Island in the Shannon, when pictures were created in the mind that will never be erased ...

W E DID NOT have a camera that day. There are no photographs but I have the pictures. Those in my memory will remain with me forever to brighten up the dark days.

Let me take you on a picnic. 1948 – the first sunny Sunday that summer. Our little boat smells of fresh tar as we push out onto the Abbey River from Athlunkard Boat Club in Limerick city and head upstream to St. Thomas' Island on the Shannon. Our timing is bad as there is a slight ebb tide and the rowing is tough.

Mam waves to us as she crosses O'Dwyer Bridge pushing the big pram and carrying a white confectionary box with Troy's Bakery emblazoned on it. She will meet us again at the end of the Mill Road.

No sooner is she out of earshot than Dad begins singing –

Aaaa ... yoke yam

Aaaa ... yoke yam

'The song of the Volga Boatmen,' Dad pauses to announce. 'We're Russian fishermen on our way to catch sturgeon for caviar. Pull harder on those oars, me hearties.'

Aaaa ... yoke yam. 'C'mon sing with me. It'll help you. See the song is the timing for rowing.'

Aaaa ... yoke yam.

Sure enough the chant provides us with the rhythm to row and we join in the singing as we slice through bulrushes by the side of the river, startling a few coot and water hens from their nests. And in between the singing Dad regales us with tales of the prowess of Cossack horsemen and romantic stories of Russian Royals living in exile in Paris. And there is another song –

At the Balalaika where there is magic in the sparkling wine and mellow music in the candles shine, I have a rendezvous.

In no time at all we're gliding through the ruined columns of the Lax Weir and come to land at the cove of St. Thomas' Island. Dad puts us ashore and takes the boat across the river to pick up Mam and the baby at the appointed place – the old mill – while we wade through masses of tall buttercups carrying the picnic bags on our heads. We crush stems of river-mint with our bare feet and the scent is hmmm ..., so fragrant.

Mam settles herself in the shade of the chestnut tree with her knitting. My brother goes to fill the blackened kettle from the Shannon.

Dad does his boyscout-firelighting thing humming '*At the Balalaika*' and Mam joins in high soprano – '*I hear a violin, a haunting gypsy violin ...*' while the baby gurgles beside her. My job is to fix the glass lemonade bottles full of milk into the mud of the cool shallows making sure that the newspaper stoppers remain above the water. The scent of wood smoke greets me on my return to our picnic place.

A thread of blue smoke rises from the crackling sticks and Dad tells us to watch out for the genie that'll jump out someday to grant us three wishes.

'You're filling their heads with nonsense,' Mam says, halting the clickity click of her needles to cluck 'Tsk. Tsk. Tsk.'

Lunch is smoky tea made in the blackened kettle that deposits an inch of tea-leaves in our enamel mugs. There are thick slices of Tubridy's cottage bread smothered in Mam's gooseberry jam and then, the *Piece de Resistance:* the Troy's confectionary box is opened to reveal a clutch of snow-white meringues. It is a meal fit for a king or a queen.

Sometime later my brother and I, armed with dinner forks, go searching for eels in the rocky part of the river. We walk out into the water wearing our runners for protection from the sharp edges and we overturn flat stones to reveal their hiding places.

I dread the thought of spearing an eel, but I do. It clasps tightly around my wrist and all I want to do is scream and scream but I must not, I must be brave. I hold my breath and run all the way back and drop the fish at Thomas Clancy's feet. He's the only person who eats eel.

Did you ever smell an eel frying? Did you ever see it squirm while it is cooking? I don't know which is worse.

When the rooks return, cawing, to the tall trees in Ruddock's garden, it is time to pack up and go. Mam is ferried back to the Mill Road where she retrieves the pram and tucks the baby in for the long walk home. We float downriver on a lazy ebb tide and now there is no need to call in the Volga Boatmen for rhythm.

The river reflects the golden sunset as Dad reads aloud from his book, *The Brothers Karamazov*, pausing now and then to hum a tune, which he tells us is an old Russian folk song called *Kalinka*.

The pictures are in my memory bank accompanied by the sloshing, sighing sound of the river lapping against the boat.

I can even feel the sting of my sunburned arms and the echo of our voices as we drift under the Metal Bridge.

Come to think of it, I'm glad there was no camera to take photographs that day; I have far better pictures in my mind.

Mae Leonard now lives in Naas, Co. Kildare but is a native of Limerick and that city features in many of her stories and recollections, which have been published in many outlets. She has appeared a number of times in the Ireland's Own Anthologies *and is a regular contributor to the* Ireland's Own *magazine and to Sunday Miscellany on RTÉ radio.*

The Long March

By Brian McCabe,
Naas, Co. Kildare

A young man and his colleagues have been busily preparing for months and then the word they had been eagerly awaiting arrived – the orders had come from Dublin. They were to march into the city on Sunday morning. Then it was all off, and next day it was on again and they marched off to join in The Rising.

I REMEMBER THERE was total confusion about it at the time. It was what we had been planning and training for, for at least a year. All those marches and manoeuvres – up and down and over and back, hail, rain or shine, day or night, carrying our packs, loading and unloading our weapons. We had been told that the order would come soon, and that we would have to be ready to go at a moment's notice.

And now it was finally here. The orders had actually come from Dublin – or so we were told. We were to march in to the city on the Sunday morning. We assembled in the yard of our commander's shop. He sold hardware and drapery, but he also stored our weapons out the back in one of his sheds.

We got ready to break out the guns and ammunition. Just then, a motor bike roared into the yard and the dusty rider handed a dispatch to our leader. He perused it quickly and I could see his face fall as he read. 'Boys', he said 'It's been called off. We are to stand down.' But I could see he was not happy. After a moment, he addressed us again: 'Don't anyone leave

166

the district tonight. I'm going to go into the city myself and find out what's happening'.

We dispersed, talking among ourselves. I don't think anyone slept very much that night. First thing next morning, after a rushed breakfast, I went back up to the shop to see what might be happening. The shutters were down and the shop was closed. I went around the back. Our commander was busy loading bags with buckshot and I could see that he had taken our weapons out of their hiding places.

'It's on,' he said simply.

Soon we had assembled again. This time, there were a few drop-outs, but never mind, there was still fifteen of us, and our orders were to meet up with other units as we proceeded.

When everything was ready, we marched off in formation – our spirits high. To throw the police off the scent, we marched down the town in the wrong direction. We didn't want them to know we were going to Dublin. They probably thought it was just another of our route marches. I glanced at the familiar shop fronts as I marched along. How long would it be until I saw them again – if ever?

When we got to the back gate of the College, we marched on along the canal bank about a mile or so out of the town. When we got to the bridge, we changed direction again and marched along the railway line, heading for the rendezvous point. Reaching there, we laid down our packs and sat down.

I was glad of the rest. My new boots, that I had bought just a few weeks before, were a bit tight and I was worried that they might soon start to hurt my feet.

We waited for what seemed like hours, but there was no sign of the other unit which we were supposed to meet. Our commander conferred with the second-in-command. After a few minutes, he addressed us again: 'We can't wait any longer

167

lads. We have to press on. It looks like we may be on our own. If anyone wants to drop out now and head back home, we won't think any less of him.'

No one left.

We picked up our gear, shouldered it, and headed off. After a few minutes, one of the lads started to hum a marching tune and soon we all joined in. There was no going back now.

By the time we reached the edge of the city, it was getting near dusk and my feet were now really beginning to hurt. Thankfully, at that point our commander called a halt. There was a railway bridge ahead and he wanted to check out whether it was safe to proceed. Oddly, we had not heard or seen any trains on the line since we began our march. After a few minutes, our scouts came back to report that there was no sign of the enemy, so on we marched.

Just as we reached the outskirts of the city, the rain began. First as a light drizzle but it soon deepened to a heavier downpour. We did have rain gear for our marches but most of us, in the excitement, had headed off without it that morning. As the rain dripped down my back and into my boots, I told myself that at least it would ease my sore feet.

On we marched, past the first cluster of houses, but soon we left the road and headed towards the canal again. Once again, our commander called a halt. Thinking that we were camping for the night, we started to unroll our packs. 'No' he said, 'This is just a short break. We must press on. They need us in Dublin as soon as possible and, anyway, we'll be safer travelling at night. The patrols won't pick us up'.

Those who had brought food, and something to drink, shared it with the others. A quick smoke and we were on the move again. Now we really did feel like soldiers.

On we trudged along the towpath, and soon we thought we could hear the sounds of gunfire in the distance. It seemed to me that there was a sort of glow on the horizon when I glanced ahead, but mostly I just kept my head down and concentrated on where I was putting my feet. My mother's childhood admonitions about not going too close to the canal banks came back to me and I smiled grimly.

Oh mother, if you could see me now!

After another hour or so, the commander ordered us to turn right. 'I'm glad someone knows where we're going' I thought to myself as we wheeled right. Soon we were marching across, of all things, a golf course. The man ahead of me marched around one of the manicured greens, careful not to walk on the closely cropped grass, and I followed him in turn, our feet leaving wet prints in the longer grass.

By now, dawn was beginning to redden along the horizon and the rain had, thankfully, stopped. So did our troop. Ahead lay the swollen waters of the river. 'Now what?' I asked myself.

There was no question of a detour at this stage. Our commander ordered us to cross as quickly and quietly as we could. Dutifully we waded in, our weapons held high above our heads, the waters reaching to our waist, as we put one foot carefully in front of another. Several times I felt my feet slip under me on the muddy bed of the river and I had a sudden vision of myself being swept off downstream, with my companions vainly trying to catch me as I hurtled by.

My uniform, which had begun to dry out, was now totally soaking again. I consoled myself with the thought that I could hardly get any wetter than I already was.

We all reached the other side safely and off we set again. Soon I could see the looming walls of the old cemetery, and that is where we finally stopped. 'It's getting light now,' the commander said. 'This is where we'll stop and rest'. And that's what we did.

The commander posted guards (thankfully I was not chosen) and the rest of us settled down to sleep as best we could.

I awoke to the sound of gunfire; much louder and sounding closer now. I shivered as I realised what lay ahead of us. The reality of what we had undertaken had begun to sink in.

The commander had been out to *reconnoitre* already and reported back that the way into the city seemed clear. Out we marched along the road. By now my right foot was throbbing and I thought briefly about taking off my boot, but I knew that if I did that, there was no way I would be able to march down to the city centre with the others. Biting my lip, I marched on stoically.

As we neared the first canal bridge, we spotted two men in uniform. We stopped immediately and ran for cover. After a few moments, we realised that the uniforms they were wearing were the same as ours.

Cautiously, we approached and told them our story. They were incredulous when we told them where we had marched from. They told us that the fighting was now fierce down in the city and that they were glad to have been posted up there on picket duty. They invited us to join them, but our commander said we must report down to headquarters for orders.

Now we could march openly, in formation, with our heads held high. Whistling, we proceeded down the strangely empty streets. As we marched, we could see some of the residents peeping out of their houses. Some shouted at us to turn back, that we would be slaughtered; others jeered, and some were just curious. Occasionally, there was a wave or a cheer from a door or a window.

On we marched, down towards the Monument, standing tall at the end of the long wide street, the rising sun shining off its polished surface. Now we knew, for sure, that we would actually make it.

The pain in my right foot seemed to fade.

Suddenly, there was a volley of shots to the left and bullets whizzed around us. One howled off the wall beside me and I felt something like a tug at my leg. I glanced down and saw a neat hole through the bottom of the leg of my uniform. Another inch and it would have taken my leg off!

We dived for cover behind the comforting bulk of the stone monument and waited. After a few minutes, when there was no sign of further fire, we cautiously stuck our heads around the corner. The street was silent, and empty. In the distance I could see what looked like the dead body of a horse, lying half on and half off the footpath.

Rapidly, we advanced down the street, running from doorway to doorway, as we had done in training so many times. No further shots came, and now we were down under the great looming colonnades of the Post Office.

The door opened and I could see a man in uniform standing just inside. We dashed in, still fearful of another fusillade. The man advanced with his hand out. 'You are most welcome' he smiled and his broad face, with its full moustache, beamed with delight. I recognised him from the photographs I had seen in the papers – Commandant James Connolly, no less!

We had made it!

Brian McCabe is a retired civil servant, originally from Co. Cavan, now living in Co Kildare. He is a regular contributor to Ireland's Own *and various other historical and archaeological journals, including* History Ireland *and* Archaeology Ireland. *More recently he has turned his hand to creative writing, and has had several short stories and poems published, and won a runners-up prize in the* Ireland's Own Original Writing Competition 2013.

Going to Boarding School

By Lourdes Mackey,
St. Patrick's Hill, Cork city

*Preparing with a mixture of trepidation and excitement for
beginning in September a new life in a whole new world
at boarding school ...*

'KINSALE' I HEARD said, 'that's where you're going, to the convent, the Sisters of Mercy.' Kinsale! I didn't know it. I didn't know any of the towns we sang off in geography. I'd only ever been into Cork City on the bus, on some Saturdays. My sixth-class history book told me that Kinsale was a fishing town in the southwest, ravaged by the Famine. But the Famine was a long time ago.

As for nuns! I'd knelt beside a nun at Mass, once. She was visiting her sister, home from the Missions – all black and white and starched, smelling of soap, and eyes closed, feeding heavy black beads through thumb and pointing-finger. But I'd not spoken to her. I'd never spoken to a nun.

The letter arrived in the post. I well remember the day. 'Looks important,' Danny-the-Post said, handing the bulging envelope to my mother.

'Tis typed.'

Printed on plush blue vellum, the gold letterhead read:
Our Lady of the Rosary Boarding School for Girls, Convent of Mercy, Kinsale. Dated July 1st, it was signed by Sister Mary

Immaculata. Listed in the reams of what was required were the names of the retailers that sold the uniform.

My mother prayed that it wouldn't be too dear, I prayed for a blazer and gymslip like the one Marion Moore wore to South Pres. We needed double everything: two blouses, two nightdresses (no pyjamas), two pairs of flat black shoes and heavy fawn tights, sanitary towels (no tampons).

The lady in the Munster Arcade produced a grey tweed skirt, way below my knee and a short box jacket, edged with blue piping. 'Kinsale blue,' she purred ...'this is the new uniform. They had a navy gymslip and blazer, but changed to this lovely suit. Isn't it stylish?'

'It's a costume,' I wailed at my mother outside, 'and so crabbit.'

'Quiet,' she hissed, 'we can barely afford it.'

I wanted to kill my mother.

My full name had to go on everything – every collar and edge, even on the cutlery. 'Not a spoon can you lose,' my mother warned, 'your Aunt Aggie had them specially engraved in Egan's. So expensive!'

Oh great! I thought. Five years of minding knives and forks. And of course, the schoolbooks: 'The letter said that I can buy them new in the school bookshop when I arrive,' I reminded her.

Then I listened to thunder, as my mother listed the sacrifices made to send me to boarding school – holding up one finger after another in support of her detailed data. 'You'll have second-hand like your brother and be glad of it,' she chided and then spent Saturday mornings trawling through second-hand bookshops. I spent Saturday evenings erasing and writing over past owners' names and doodles.

I wanted to kill my mother.

'Just a trim,' she said, but I fancied my hair long like the girls in *Jackie* magazine. 'Get a bob like the one in Maxi, Dick and Twink,' Marion Moore suggested. I told this to the hairdresser but she didn't listen to me. She listened to my mother. Then, I looked like Nonie Cremin in fifth class, who had the same pudding bowl haircut as her brothers.

I wanted to kill my mother.

The day in September arrived and we loaded my new acquisitions into Pakie Barry's Ford Anglia. My brother tried to rise me.

'You'll be just like the internees in the North,' he teased, 'locked up without a trial.'

But I didn't fall for it.

'No, it'll be like St. Trinian's or the Four Marys,' I bragged, 'all midnight feasts and high jinks after lights out.'

A grey, multi-eyed building stood on the hill, supervising the town. The car corkscrewed along the narrow streets until at last we arrived at the boarding school entrance. When the Anglia had disgorged my belongings, Pakie Barry grabbed my hand and said:

'Mind yerself now girl, and watch them nuns, they're jades, just don't let um best ye.'

Tears brimmed. My mother, trying to plámás me, soothed; 'Come on now, here's your box of goodies for those famous midnight feasts.' Clutching the box, I made my way to the first-year dormitory.

The smell of floor polish dry-fogged my nostrils. I looked at the row of beds and then at the row of strange faces. Loneliness like measles flew from one of us to the next. I stood at the window, and sad as the last swallow, watched the Ford Anglia carry my mother away until it was a tiny speck.

I wanted my mother.

The girl sitting on the next bed smiled and offered me a Mikado biscuit. 'My name is Margaret,' she said. 'What's yours?'

We crunched the biscuits and started to chat. Soon we were giggling.

We are still chatting and giggling.

Lourdes Mackey is currently a teacher living in Cork. Her non-fiction has been published in various journals and newspapers including the Irish Times *and the* Irish Examiner. *She has contributed to RTÉ's Sunday Miscellany and to the art and culture website Headstuff. Her short fiction was placed third in the 2016 Colm Toibín International Short Story Competition.*

The Solution

By Siobhan Flynn,
Clonroche, Co. Wexford

An old couple approach advancing age and ill health on an isolated farm on the side of the mountain after sharing a lifetime of toil and hard work. He is not well but desperate to stay at home; she is driven to thinking of even more desperate solutions ...

RISING STIFFLY FROM a battered armchair, Mary Anne McTiernan deftly flipped open the hotplate of the old Aga cooker and shoved another log into the smouldering embers. The log, green and sappy, hissed and oozed, and would provide little enough heat. She would have to ring Declan Doherty in the morning to order more coal, and listen to him grumbling, as usual, about the state of the driveway. She would have to hold her tongue, since Doherty's was the only place in town that would deliver out this far.

Seated again, she lifted her mug of tepid tea. All day long she had fretted and it was now approaching midnight. With some reluctance, she decided against a small shot of whiskey – she needed to think and for that she needed a clear head.

Outside, the wind had picked up. Occasionally a clatter of hail rattled on the window panes. It was the rain that had done most of the damage over the years, insinuating its way through the places on the roof where slates had gone missing, causing damp and mould in the upstairs rooms and creating rivulets of water on the window ledges where the frames were rotted and warped. But it was the wind that bothered her more, lately. It wasn't unlike the cry of an animal, she thought, progressing gradually from a low moan to a high-pitched shriek. Anything could be loose out there on the side of that mountain, if you were to believe the wind.

A few months short of her seventy-second birthday, Mary Anne bore the appearance of a woman ten years older. A lifetime of outdoor work and exposure to harsh weather had loosened and dried the skin of her face, making it as limp and baggy as an old sock. Her thick grey hair was coarse and unkempt. In her youth she had been wiry and vigorous, now her thinness was accentuated by the drooping of what little flesh covered her long bones. In truth, she felt ancient, as ancient as the mountains that overlooked the remote farm, older than the rocks from which the stone house had been hewn.

On nights such as this one, old aches resurfaced – injuries sustained while working the land; arthritis in her fingers slowed her in her tasks, chilblains on her feet made the cold unbearable and the heat nearly worse. And yet, looking back, she couldn't imagine a different life, or imagine having wanted anything other than what she had had.

Against the howl of the wind she cocked her ear suddenly to a sound from within the house, before rising again and creaking open the door to the hall.

Clutching her tattered layers against the draught she made her way up the sagging steps to the small room at the top of the stairs, calling softly as she entered, 'Are you all right, Barty?' repeating the question when there was no immediate response.

The coughing had stopped, but her husband's rasping breath was almost as painful to listen to. The air was heavy with the odours of illness – Vick ointment and camphor oil, stale bedclothes, old tea and underlying dampness.

The room was not warm by any standards, but by comparison to the rest of the house it appeared quite snug. A small electric heater provided this modicum of heat. On the narrow bed, subsided breathlessly on the grubby pillows, he answered her with some difficulty.

'Aye, aye … I'm ok now.'

Slowly, Mary Anne lowered herself onto the chair beside the bed, reaching for his gnarled old hand. Today had been one of his better days, earlier he had had a little porridge and a drop of soup. For almost a week now he hadn't been out of bed, except, with her help, to visit the lavatory.

'Would you take a sup, Barty? Would we take a little sup together?' She had a longing now for the shot of whiskey, that flame in her throat to banish the cold and the despair.

'Aye … maybe I would'.

But even as he spoke, his eyes drooped again in sleep, his breathing became less laboured, so there was nothing for it but to slip away quietly. On her way back to the kitchen she caught a shadowy glimpse of herself in the dusty, mottled hall mirror – a hunched old scarecrow of a woman – and she felt a peculiar urge to laugh, though nothing was in the least funny.

The farm and the house had been a windfall of sorts – her inheritance from an elderly bachelor uncle. In the early years there had been pleasure in the hard work, and even as time went by and no children arrived to assist them, she and Barty had toiled on, side by side. They were private people, neither of them having much in the way of relatives; their neighbours out on the hills, working people like themselves, had little enough time for socializing.

Having twice been stricken with TB as a young man, Barty had never been as robust as she was herself, succumbing easily to various ailments, growing more frail in late middle age. Things had become difficult then. No matter how hard Mary Anne worked there had never been enough time or money, and the farm and the house assumed an air of neglect, which continued to become more pronounced year on year. Eventually, the stock had had to go; the few bob they got from the lease of the field was what they lived on now. It was Mary Anne who held together what little they had left, and so far she had managed.

The problem was the District Nurse, a woman named Agnes Copeland. Everything had been simple before she had started making her calls, poking about the place, interfering in their lives. A well-heeled woman from the town, what could she possibly know about the toughness of life lived on a hillside farm, about the endless work, the wet, the cold and the hardship, about the whims of the weather and stubbornness of the rocky soil, about surviving regardless?

Since Barty's health had taken a turn for the worse, she had been arriving more frequently, tapping smartly on the yard door, sometimes letting herself in before Mary Anne had a chance to admit her.

Two days previously, Mary Anne had been alerted by the noise of the small car labouring its way up the steep, rutted drive. By the time the nurse had picked her way through the mud of the yard, Mary Anne was waiting on the door step in front of the closed door.

Their initial greeting had been cordial enough, though Mary Anne knew that the nurse considered her difficult and uncooperative.

'And how is Barty, then?' she had enquired, 'Any improvement in the chest?'

179

'Actually, he's been better the last couple of days, up and about a bit'.

Mary Anne had nodded several times, giving emphasis to this lie.

The nurse had nodded in response, stepping forward with a tight smile, 'I'll just pop in and see him then.'

'Eh. no … it's not a good time … he's having a bit of a bath now … if you don't mind.'

'Mary Anne,' the younger woman's voice had a querulous, whining quality, her long pale face wore a pained look. 'Your husband is a sick man – he might be better off in the hospital. At least let me in to see him!'

'No. I'm after telling you, he's better, he's in the bath – and I need to keep an eye!'

The nurse had paused uncertainly, her face blank and un-readable, then to Mary Anne's surprise and relief, abruptly bade her goodbye and left. The relief, however, would be short-lived. Mary Anne knew people like Agnes Copeland could never leave well enough alone, like a type of snake she was, waiting to strike.

Later, as she had coaxed Barty to drink a little soup, he had interrupted her suddenly, his pale eyes alert and wary.

'She was here again, wasn't she?' he had queried anxiously.

'I put the skids under her, don't worry!'

She had known she wasn't fooling him. With surprising strength, he had grasped her arm as she had fussed with the rumpled blankets.

'Promise me, Mary Anne, that you won't let them put me in that hospital! That you won't let them take me away? Will you promise me now?'

'Amn't I after promising you fifty times already, Barty?' Fear and dread combined, making her voice unintentionally harsh.

Alone in the long January night, a plan of sorts had been hatching in her feverish brain; a way in which they might reach a solution to the problem of Agnes Copeland. This plan was more of a fantasy than anything – an idea that had sprung from a TV programme they had seen recently, involving the discovery of human remains in remote areas and the efforts by the authorities to identify them. She had idly remarked that there could be any number of bodies buried in the heavily forested mountainside behind their farm, without a hope of ever being found.

In the wall cupboard beside the Aga, Barty's rifle stood, wrapped carefully in a piece of candlewick bedspread. He had taught her to shoot many years ago in the old quarry, for her own protection he had said, and to keep down vermin around the place.

Much to his amusement, she had turned out to be a crack-shot, with a keen sharp eye and a steady, accurate aim; though she herself had been oddly uncomfortable with this new skill.

In her imagination now, she saw the nurse's car pull into their yard. The next thing she saw was that car, driven by herself, under cover of darkness, up the steep, rocky road through the forest, deeper and deeper, to the point where the pine branches scraped the sides and roof of the car, and the dimmed headlights cut a funnel through the murky gloom. Beside her in the car was the slumped, lifeless body of the nurse. Thereafter, Mary Anne imagined her own painstaking journey back through the forest, on foot, by torchlight. At dawn, it started to snow, a heavy fall that kept the area inaccessible for weeks.

The search for the missing woman would be ongoing, but no one would ever suspect a harmless old pair of hermits, with no possible motive for wanting to harm anybody. It would take months, amid all the furore, to replace the District Nurse, by which time it would be summer, and she herself would have nursed Barty back to health.

The problem with this plan was that her imagination could not – even with a shot of whiskey inside her – summon up the details of the piece in the middle. She was unable to visualize the perpetration of the act itself. She saw a shadowy image of herself, concealed behind the ragged curtain at the landing window as the nurse drove into the yard, but like an old Polaroid photograph, it was blurred and insubstantial.

In reality she was terrified of the rifle, could not even bring herself to take it out of the cupboard, did not even like the fact that it was there at all but was all too aware of it at the same time. It lurked under its innocuous wrapping, gleaming with cold potential, a can of worms, daring someone to open it. It could be rusted to bits for all she knew, or cared. Only it wasn't rusted, it was snug there in its hiding place, the warmest spot in the house, patiently biding its time.

Mary Anne realized she was crying now, not just weeping but crying in earnest, the tears oozing from her eyes and coursing down her withered cheeks. It was almost 2.00 a.m., the fire was dead, and the elements buffeting the windows like lost souls begging admission. No wonder her brain was tired and befuddled. It was time to leave off thinking for tonight.

Tomorrow she would surely come up with a solution.

Wexford-born, Siobhan Flynn lives in Clonroche with her husband Joe, two teenage daughters, an elderly collie and an energetic terrier. She works with Wexford County Council. She has had two short stories published previously, in Irelands Own *magazine. She has also had poetry published in* The Leitrim Guardian *and other local publications.*

An Ordinary Sunday

DEIRDRE MANNING,
BARNA ROAD, GALWAY

*A typical, reasonably prosperous Irish family is one of the
many caught up in the turmoil of the fall-out from the Celtic
Tiger era and things have come to a head. The mother takes the
dog for a walk around their familiar local haunts as she
reflects on life and times in the new Ireland.*

FOR OUR NEIGHBOURS it's an ordinary Sunday but not for us. We have been listening to a programme on the radio about the Great War. The contributors include well-known journalists and politicians. They are enjoying the discussion and are already setting the scene for a commemoration of the Easter Rising which is still some two years away.

Coincidentally, both my grandfather and my husband's grandfather were involved in these events. Mine was involved in the Easter Rising and his in the Great War.

'I'll take Rebel for a walk,' I say as I head for the door.

'Ok. I'll finish up here.' The timbre of my husband's voice reflects our situation. The dog, a cocker spaniel with baleful eyes and an exuberant disposition, bounds out the door with an enthusiasm that only a dumb animal could muster in the circumstances.

He strains on the leash as we walk towards the sports fields and the wood which is our favourite route. It is a beautiful summer evening. I smile a greeting at a neighbour. She is

German and very reserved. Though we have been neighbours for nearly fourteen years we are only on nodding terms.

The dog and I pass a bus stop where Spanish students are gathered, chatting animatedly and showing each other the latest news on their smartphones. I get off the footpath, to give them a wide berth, in case Rebel decides to make a lunge for a dangling headphone. When we reach the sports fields I release him from the leash and he shoots off like a grey-hound out of trap.

There are a number of young men playing football on the soccer pitch. They are wearing football shirts with names such as Messi and Suarez. I look in vain for a Keane or Duff but they're already outdated. Among the bramble and briars there are swathes of convolvulus and some thistle, swaying gently in the south westerly breeze.

A butterfly lands, silently on the head of a dandelion. By contrast, bees are buzzing noisily and a maiden fly is in full graceful flight. Then I see it – a perfect ladybird making its way down a blade of grass. A poem learnt in childhood comes to mind:

'The beauty of the world hath made me sad,
This beauty that will pass;
Sometimes my heart hath shaken with great joy
To see a leaping squirrel in a tree,
Or a red lady-bird upon a stalk …'

I feel the tears welling up in my eyes but I dare not let them flow. I walk on.

In what is normally a Gaelic pitch, a group of dark skinned young men are playing cricket. I'm no linguist but I think they are speaking Urdu. I look at them and think of my grandfather. In his wildest dreams he wouldn't have imagined his granddaughter encountering people of three different nationalities less than a five-minute walk from home.

Although an enthusiastic GAA fan and a county player he would have approved of this turn of events – local community facilities catering for everybody. He had become a pacifist and had mellowed significantly by the time I got to know him. My husband's grandfather might have been equally surprised. He too belonged to a very different world. Both grandfathers survived their separate wars but each had a brother who didn't.

My husband and I often spoke about our grandfathers in the early years of our relationship, in the years when we thought we couldn't know enough about each other. There was often banter about their very different choices. We could turn any domestic argument laughingly into a slanging match about my grandfather, the glorified rabble-rouser, or his grandfather who failed to see the irony of fighting 'for the freedom of small nations' in the army of a country which was occupying his own small nation.

Eventually, we would collapse in paroxysms of laughter on the sofa having forgotten what the original row was about. We were well aware of the complicated political situation which existed in the early part of the 20th century in Ireland but we never gave it any serious thought. It was history.

I walk further towards the wood. My friend is walking in my direction with her autistic son, Timmy. He is sixteen now and nearly a man. He doesn't acknowledge me, but he crouches down beaming to rub the dog which joyfully licks his face. His mother is a bit embarrassed.

'When are you off then?' she asks.

'Tomorrow!' I'll bring the dog over in the morning.' The only good thing about our situation is that I will be giving Rebel to them. Timmy loves him and his mother has been advised that a dog could be good for him. But Rebel is aptly named and might need some retraining.

'I'll miss you and not only because you're great with Timmy.'

'I'll try and help out again once we're settled,' I say, though I'm far from sure that this will be possible and she knows that.

'Don't you be worrying about us,' she smiles. She looks at her son and the dog, both clearly delighted to see each other. I can see that she is anxious to escape. I put the dog's leash back on and haul him away. Timmy stops smiling.

In the wood it's cooler. We walk the well-worn path and come out the other end into the sunshine. I decide to go to the beach. It's about another ten minutes. The tide is in and I have to keep the dog on the leash because dogs aren't allowed run free on the beach between 8 a.m. and 8 p.m. during the summer months.

I went for a swim this morning at 7.30. I thought I would have the beach to myself but there were two other swimmers. I grimaced at them as I allowed the cold water to creep up my body, seeping coldly through my swim suit. I eventually took the plunge when the water reached my ribs. I came up gasping. I dived again and for twenty minutes I swam back and forth across the beach – fast urgent strokes at first before the calm water lulled me and my strokes became more languid and I relaxed.

For a short while I was able to forget. But before I had dried myself completely I was back to reality. Now I sit on a large rock and contemplate the situation in which I find myself. The dog sits beside me and looks out to sea as if he's expecting his boat to come in.

The sea road could be in the middle of the country. In places you can't see a house even though just over the brow of the hill there are several suburban housing estates. I walk slowly. The dog is no longer straining on the leash as if he knows what's before him. He loves Timmy but he might miss us. Even though he's only three years old, I will really miss him and my daughter is heartbroken at the thought of losing him.

As I turn off the main road into our street, I admire the gardens. There's berberis, hydrangea, fuchsia and even some of the dreaded leylandia, with its dual effect of blocking out the light and the neighbours. There are colourful flower beds and well-manicured lawns.

Some of the neighbours are tending their gardens in the unusually good weather. I nod at those I don't know well and hope that those I know better won't be in their gardens. I'm fed up with the sympathetic glances, the uncertain smiles, the feeling that they're relieved that it isn't them.

'Are you going racing next week?' A tall man with a friendly face and receding hair asks as he stops washing his car to chat. He has only recently moved in and I have never spoken to him before.

'Not this year,' I say, not wanting to get involved in a conversation. 'We're moving out this week.'

'That's a pity,' he replies. 'I was hoping for a few tips.'

'Not from me I'm afraid.' I walk on and he returns to his task.

As I walk the last few yards I notice that most houses have two good cars outside. Funny, that never registered with me before. Turning into our drive I wonder how much longer our ten-year-old runabout will last. We have been living frugally on the proceeds of the sale of a five-year-old Lexus for quite a while now.

When I open the door I can smell the casserole that I put on earlier. It's an unseasonable meal but it's a family favourite and it's cheap. I have made a fresh fruit salad and bought some posh ice cream for dessert. I even splashed out on a bottle of plonk.

I pick my way through the packing cases in the hall and the kitchen. My husband looks at me over his shoulder. The life is gone from his eyes and little wonder. Our business collapsed some time ago – not because we couldn't get work but because we couldn't get paid. One after the other those that owed us money went to the wall. We held out to the bitter end. We managed to pay off the staff but we're owed a fortune and we haven't paid our mortgage for several years. The life we worked so hard to build is gone.

'What's there to celebrate?' our daughter asks coming into the room.

'This family,' I reply, trying to be cheerful. 'We have each other. We may be at rock bottom now but the only way is up.'

'You hope,' she says with a small uncertain smile. She's the one I'm most worried about. We have about a month to sort out our welfare entitlements and try and find a house for rent, that we can afford, before she goes back to school. In the interim we will move in with my parents, fifty miles away. I really want to move back to this area so that she won't have to change schools.

She's trying not to add to our problems by articulating her fears. Her brother is hoping that he did OK in the Leaving Certificate. If that all goes well he will get a grant for University.

In the meantime we are practically destitute. The red tape is horrendous. It's made more difficult by the fact that we were self-employed. You fill out one form and then there's another. There are photocopies to be got, certificates to be presented, our accounts for years past. To be fair the person behind the hatch is quite nice, but we get the impression she's bored. We haven't been bored since we became desperate.

We'll be handing the keys into the bank tomorrow. They will let us have anything that is left over from the proceeds of the sale but we're not holding our breath. It's quite likely that we will still owe them money after the sale. They advertised it on-line some time ago and had no interest so far. We had never heard the term 'negative equity' until we were in it.

Our son comes into the kitchen carrying two framed pictures.

'Look at what I found on top of my wardrobe,' he says puzzled.

He shows us the sepia photos of two young men, their soldiers' uniforms uncannily similar, each carrying a rifle, going to a different war. The photos are faded, the frames shabby.

'Who are they?'

'Actually they're your great grandfathers – that's your Dad's grandfather and that's mine!' I say pointing to the pictures. I really don't want to give him a lesson on recent Irish history now. I want to sit down and eat. But I'm thinking that neither of those young men was thinking about negative equity, when they were putting their lives on the line for future generations.

Deirdre Manning recently retired as manager of an information centre. She has three adult children and lives in Galway. She has been writing as a hobby for many years. In 2013, writing as Miranda Manning, her novel Who is Alice? *was published by Poolbeg. In 2014 she came second in the Irish Writers Union James Plunkett Memorial Award and was published in the* Ireland's Own Original Irish Writing Anthology.

An Unforgettable November Evening

By Maura O'Sullivan,
Tramore, Co. Waterford

The evening of November 22, 1963 and all is right with my world.
Dad reads the paper as a coal fire warms the room, while Mam
heads off to her church devotions. Little did we know that within
minutes an event thousands of miles away would
reverberate around the world …

I WAS FEELING perfectly content on that November evening. I was seven years old. My Dad sat in his armchair engrossed in the *Irish Independent.* He occasionally looked up to check the sports programme on the black and white television.

A coal fire warmed the small room. The scent of newly washed clothes, airing on a clothes horse, filled the air. I sat on the hearth playing with my doll. She had a very pretty yellow dress and, most importantly, long hair which was styled and restyled continuously. She was given to me as a special present on the occasion of my First Holy Communion the previous May.

My Mam had gone to devotions in the local church with some of the neighbours. She tied her headscarf under her chin and reminded us to keep the fire going while she was gone.

Dad put down the newspaper when an announcer interrupted the television programme to tell us of a newsflash. Charles Mitchell sent the whole country into shock when he told us that President Kennedy had been shot. It was Friday, November 22nd, 1963.

That fateful night is remembered so well. My Dad stared in disbelief at the television and even as a young child I knew how terrible this news was.

Only a few months had passed since President Kennedy's visit to Ireland. He had made everyone so proud to be Irish. The achievements of an emigrant's great grandchild had lifted the hearts of a nation to the point where our sense of importance as a people on the world stage was heightened.

John Fitzgerald Kennedy was a very good looking, charming and charismatic man. So my Mam thought anyway. She was particularly excited when he visited New Ross and his ancestral home in Dunganstown, Co. Wexford as these places were close to us in Waterford.

Everyone had watched the televised coverage and listened attentively to the wireless. His speeches were warm, witty, entertaining and poignant. His broad smile and memorable words connected with all those privileged enough to hear him.

Jackie Kennedy, who was not with him on this visit, was also idolised for her beauty, chic fashion sense and style. Irish women loved to see pictures of her and studied her outfits.

My Mam amused my Dad on many occasions by reciting parts of his speeches, imitating his Boston drawl. I remember her favourite quotes:

'When my great grandfather left here to become a cooper in East Boston, he carried nothing with him except two things: a strong religious faith and a strong desire for liberty' and his last words on Irish soil, 'I'll come back and see old Shannon's face again'.

By the time my Mam arrived home from the church with two neighbours in tow, another newsflash from an emotional Charles Mitchell had informed us that the president was dead.

They had heard on their way home. People were going out on the streets to tell neighbours or passers-by the terrible news from Dallas, Texas.

Everyone was in shock.

'How could this have happened?'

'Oh poor Jackie, and she was right there with him you know, and the little children to lose such a Dad. May his soul rest in peace.'

The tears started again when they thought about his promise to 'See old Shannon's face again.'

My Mam put on the kettle as happened in all times of trouble. There were tears, tea and biscuits. Then we all knelt to say the Rosary for the repose of his soul.

A picture hung over our fireplace paying homage to the Rosary and indicating that it was recited in the house each night at eight. There were nights when it didn't happen which often prompted my Mam to say:

'I'm taking down that picture because it's just not true.'

On that night, however, there was no doubt; it had to be said.

The days that followed I remember as grim, sad and grey, where everyone felt a light had gone out in Ireland and in the whole world.

There was nothing else spoken about. On Monday we saw some television coverage of the funeral ceremony at Arlington Cemetery, Virginia. We were glad to see our president there paying his respects on behalf of us all. The vision of Jackie with her two young children has stayed with me all my life, particularly the salute of his young son on that sad day.

The memory of the night of November 22nd, 1963, brings me back to a simpler, more innocent time. Though it was a time of sadness, I was cocooned by the love of my parents, the warmth of neighbours, and the togetherness of community, facing life's tragedies but knowing that all would be well, with God's help.

Maura O'Sullivan is a retired Civil Servant, married with two sons. Her story 'Molly' was included in the 2014 Ireland's Own Anthology. She is part of Tramore Writers' Group, which has published three books of members' work.

The Magic Ring

By Mary Daly,
Dundalk, Co. Louth

Emma is proud to wear the ring that had belonged to her grandmother and her mother before her. Her mother had always told her it was a magic ring that had the gift of happiness and gave it to her when she became engaged …

EMMA LOOKED AT the engagement ring on her finger. It had been her mother's engagement ring and her mother's before that. It was her ring now. Emma had always admired the ring with its small but sparkling diamond. As a young girl, she had sat on her mother's knee and listened with the wondrous enthusiasm of a happy childhood as her mother had told her that the ring was magic.

'Is it really magic?' asked the young Emma.

'Yes,' smiled her mother, 'it has great magic.'

'What can it do?'

'The ring's magic is the gift of happiness.'

'But I am already happy' said Emma who was a little crestfallen. She had hoped, at the very least, that it could get her a pony for Christmas.

Sensing her daughter's disappointment, Emma's mother held her closer and said:

'The ring's diamond was a gift to your grandfather for saving a young soldier during the Great War. The young man had rushed forward without thinking and was cut down by a

German gunner. It was a mistake that would have cost him his life but for your grandfather bravely leaving the trenches and dragging him back to safety. When the war was over, the soldier's mother looked for your grandfather and gave him the diamond in grateful thanks. She told him that it would bring him luck and one day save him or one of his own from a great mistake.'

'And did it bring him luck?' Emma asked earnestly.

'Why yes,' replied her mother smiling. He met my mother and she had me and when it was my time I met your father and we have you.'

Emma's beautiful blue eyes opened wide 'Will I get the ring too?'

'Yes,' said her mother as she stroked Emma's long blond hair, 'When it's your time.'

'When will that be?' asked Emma impatiently.

Her mother kissed Emma on the forehead and whispered the same words 'When it's your time.'

Now it was her time. The ring was hers. On the day of her recent engagement, her mother had taken it from her finger and given it to her with a tear in her eye and a prayer in her soul for her beloved daughter's happiness. Emma reflected on the quiet passing of the ring from her mother to her and how in time she would, God willing, pass it on to her own daughter.

Emma Kennedy was marrying Martin O'Malley. Martin was the man who had literally swept her off her feet on the dance floor the first time they met. Before meeting him, she had started to think that maybe marriage wouldn't happen for her. It wasn't because there was a shortage of suitors for her hand but none of them made her feel that it was something special that would last a lifetime.

She thought how lucky she was that Martin had come into her life even if his job meant that the time they spent together was less than she wished. However, that would change when they married, she would be moving to Dublin and they would have a wonderful life together.

It wasn't supposed to have been like that. She was supposed to marry Damien Lynch. She was the girl next door, he was the boy next door. They had been inseparable childhood friends before becoming teenage sweethearts. Then came university. He went to UCD, she went to Trinity; he studied engineering and she studied history. At first, they met every day, then every weekend, then when they were at home at Christmas and Easter and then not at all.

Emma sometimes pondered how they had drifted apart. She mused about how what once seemed almost predestined had gradually slipped away as they went from friends to lovers to irregular acquaintances.

Their lives had gone in very different directions after college. He had gone to Dubai and she had returned home to teach at her old school. She had settled into a happy routine. She had great friends in Claire and Susan, a job that she had always wanted and she now had Martin.

Marriage and motherhood were what she wanted now. She smiled and laughed quietly to herself as she thought about the words 'marriage and motherhood'. 'I better keep that to myself' she thought as she looked at her engagement ring 'or they'll be buying me a rocking chair and a shawl as wedding presents.'

Over the next few months, Emma found herself fully occupied with planning her wedding. There was so much to do. Luckily, Claire and Susan were always there to help.

As so it was, as with previous Saturdays, that the girls met up for lunch and spent the afternoon in another whirlwind of shopping and conversation about dresses, accessories and shoes. Men were not mentioned, even in passing.

However, as they enjoyed their well-earned post-shopping glass of wine, Claire said, 'I hear Damien Lynch is back in town. He bought that old house on Cragg Hill and is renovating it. Apparently, he's getting married.'

'Damien's back?' said Emma surprised at his return and even more surprised by her own strong interest in this news.

'Seems so,' said Claire, 'My brother met him last night with a beautiful brunette, an American girl called Jill.'

Susan wickedly added her contribution. 'Well, there's a turn up for the books,' she said as she looked straight at Emma, 'I always thought he preferred blondes.'

'Let's change the subject, girls,' said Emma, blushing with the embarrassment of someone hiding a guilty secret, 'I have to phone Martin, he has to work all weekend.'

Emma was too busy to notice what both of her friends had spotted. Martin seemed to be around less and less. Emma always had a reason to explain his absence; it was always the same reason – work.

What Emma had noticed, however, was that her engagement ring seemed to have lost some of its sparkle.

She polished it herself but to little avail. Only one thing for it, she thought, a professional polish at the jewellers. She would drop into Jenkins the Jeweller on Monday at lunchtime.

'Could you polish my engagement ring, please, Mr Jenkins?' asked Emma 'I would like it to be brilliant for my wedding day. I can come back later to collect it.'

Mr Jenkins took the ring and smiled 'No need to come back, I'll only be a few minutes. I know no girl likes to be parted from her engagement ring.'

True to his word, the jeweller was not long gone before returning the ring to Emma. 'That's an interesting stone' he said. 'It seemed at first that nothing would bring up its shine but then suddenly it just seemed to come to life. I had to polish it quite hard so be careful with it. Bring it back if it becomes loose.'

Not paying any great attention to the jeweller's last words, Emma glided out of the shop lost in the moment of how brightly the stone shone and walked straight into Damien Lynch.

'Hello Princess,' he said with a big smile; 'I hear you're getting married.'

Before she could answer, he added. 'Isn't that the magic engagement ring?'

Regaining her composure after the embarrassment of almost stumbling into his arms, Emma said, 'The answer to both questions is yes; I am getting married and this is my engagement ring. I am surprised you remember it.'

'Who could ever forget the magic ring?' he smiled.

'Are you teasing me, Mr Lynch?' said Emma. 'I would have thought you would have been looking for an engagement ring yourself and you getting married.'

'News sure travels fast around this town,' he laughed. 'Let's just say that reports of my impending nuptials have been greatly exaggerated. You know how it is, Emma, a girl visits for a few days and you're engaged in a week and then you're married.

'Jill is a friend of mine that I met in Dubai. We expats were a small but tight community over there. She's from the US but her family lived in this area before taking the boat to the States in the 1840s. She's a great girl but, sadly, not for me. What was it your mother always used to say:'You'll know when you know' and I'm sure that's certainly true for you with that lucky engagement ring.'

For some reason that she couldn't quite put her finger on Emma was happy that Damien was not marrying the American girl.

'But you have bought that house, haven't you, so you are staying?'

'With my stash of ill-gotten Middle Eastern gold, it was either buy the house or a spot of money laundering,' he smiled, 'and anyway, a 30 year old man has to strike out from his mother's apron strings. Apart from going around for dinner every night, watching the sport with dad and my brothers, and taking my laundry around three times a week I'll be completely my own man.'

Emma laughed. She hadn't intended to but she did. She didn't intend to say what she said next either but she did.

'You haven't changed, you poor deluded fool.'

'Less of the poor', he replied with a twinkle in his eye and a mischievous grin on his face, 'it's "you rich deluded fool" now, if you please.'

With that, he said, 'Got to go, things to do, people to see. Look after yourself, Princess.'

Then he did something Emma was not expecting. He leaned forward and kissed her on the cheek. It lasted a second but unlocked a floodgate of memories and a surge of long forgotten emotions raced to the surface. She stood still, only her head moved as her eyes followed him down the street.

She was uncertain about the encounter. 'Better to think nothing, a two-hour session with Class 6A on the politics of Renaissance Italy is enough to take one's mind off anything.'

The politics of Renaissance Italy with 35 Leaving Cert girls went as well as it could on a late October afternoon. After it, Emma felt ready for a long run. She loved running. It seemed to set her free but on this occasion she slipped on some wet leaves and fell to the ground. 'A first time for everything,' she thought as she picked herself up, 'nothing broken' and continued on her run in the rain.

With her run over, she returned home and looked forward to an energising shower and a night in front of the television catching up with the soaps and not thinking about Damien Lynch.

She turned her hand to admire her ring and then she noticed the ring was there but the diamond was not. Emma was not one to panic but the diamond was definitely missing. Her mind raced over numerous possibilities.

'How could I have lost it? Where could I have lost it?'

'Retrace your steps, Emma' she told herself. 'You had it when you changed into your running gear. You don't have it now. You lost it somewhere on the run.' Then it hit her. The diamond must have come off when she fell but finding it in the dark and the rain was surely a near impossible task.

She would phone Martin. She would tell him what happened. He would understand and be supportive. She dialled his work number as he seemed to be living in the office in recent weeks. The phone rang for only a few seconds before she heard his voice 'Martin O'Malley, Project Manager'.

'Martin, something terrible has happened. I've lost the diamond in my engagement ring,' said Emma, doing what she could to prevent her cracking voice betraying her emotional turmoil. 'I took a spill when running and it came off the ring when I hit the ground.'

There was silence. It was a cruel silence that seemed to take pleasure in its length. Then Martin spoke:

'Look, Emma, I'm very, very busy at the moment. You know that, don't you? I don't really have time for this right now.'

Emma was shocked by his tone and his words. He hadn't even asked if she was okay after her fall but she found the inner strength to say with cool determination 'I can't believe you just said that. I can't believe that you can be so uncaring about my feelings and what's important to me.'

'It's just a diamond for a ring for goodness sake. I'll buy you another one, a new one, a bigger one but I have to get back to work now. You do understand that, don't you?'

Emma had been brought up never to use bad language. She prided herself that whatever the provocation she would never, ever use bad language.

On this occasion, she broke that tradition. She broke something else too. She broke off the engagement. Furious with Martin and with herself, she grabbed her coat and stormed out of the house to look for the diamond. And then for the second time in the same day, she almost collided with Damien Lynch.

'Are you stalking me or something?' she asked angrily.

'I can see you're upset, Princess.'

'Don't Princess me. I'm not in the mood for it. Please just leave me alone.'

With that he reached into his jacket pocket and carefully placed something small in the centre of his hand. At that very second, the light of the full moon fell upon what he was holding. It was a small diamond. It was her diamond and it shone like it never shone before.

In fact, it shone almost as much as Emma's blue eyes. 'Where….how…did you find it?' she asked excitedly.

'I think it found me,' he said. 'I was on my way to my mother's and would have walked past it but it was always a dazzler and its sparkle caught my eye. I picked it up and recognised it immediately. I would have phoned you but didn't have your number so I hotfooted it around here because I know how important it is to you and how you would be feeling.'

Emma took the diamond. Its reflected light blinded her for an instant but only for an instant because now she could see everything clearly. The ring was magic. It had saved her from a terrible mistake. She looked at Damien. The diamond had been lost but only as a way to show her what she already really knew. She leaned forward and kissed him on the lips.

Some years later, Emma was putting her daughter, Abigail, to bed in the house on Cragg Hill. 'Good night, Princess,' she said.

Abigail looked at her mother and pleaded for a bedtime story. 'What story would you like, Abi?' asked Emma.

The little girl replied quickly 'The one about your ring, Mummy.'

Mary Daly is in her mid 50s and married for 25 years. She has always loved literature and marvelled at great storytelling. She has wanted to write for a long time but only recently made the necessary effort. She finds the experience exciting and fulfilling and regrets not rising to the challenge earlier. 'The Magic Ring' will forever be a favourite as it is the first story she has had published. Her other passion is the piano. She says: 'Both writing and music feed and free my creative spirit and I treasure them both.'

The Kindness
of Strangers

By Eileen Casey,
Old Bawn, Dublin

*Abandoned as a baby, Alice is raised by the nuns until at
sixteen she is brought to work for Miss Flanagan in her shop
that sells everything from sweets to bags of coal.*

ALICE, A TALL girl with a gap in her front teeth, legs like a colt and a thick ebony plait down her back, came to work for Miss Flanagan when she was sixteen years old. If frightened by that first confrontation with the old woman, it didn't show in her hazel eyes.

Curious about the shop, Alice sifted out shapes in the dimly lit interior of the sweet shop, surprised to see a miscellaneous selection of goods on the shelves, from packets of firelighters and candles to clothes-pegs and china cups. Bags of coal were also for sale, stored in a nook under the counter. This resulted in a film of fine black powder dusting the glass cabinets, where jelly babies and sugared almonds were displayed.

Miss Flanagan had sent instructions to St Agnes's Home for Girls specifying a 'strapping lass with her feet on the ground and no notions above her station; a girl who would give no trouble and from whom she would take no quarter.'

When Alice was driven the eighty miles or so to the midlands shop, it was the first time she'd travelled such a distance.

203

Up until then, all she'd had to look forward to was the Sunday afternoon walk to the nearest town when she and the other girls could only enjoy window displays.

Treats arrived at St Agnes's via Christmas parcels from charitable institutions and for a time Alice had a pen-pal of similar age who soon grew tired of reading about repetitive, boring routines.

Now here she was, under the scrutiny of an old woman with white hair scraped back in a bun, her blue eyes narrowing behind a pair of round specs. Alice fancied that a thin layer of coal-dust also coated Miss Flanagan's hair, even finding its way into the deep crevices on her face.

The old woman nodded to Sister Margaret and ushered them both into the adjoining kitchen where tea was laid out on an oilcloth covered with sandwiches and cakes. The one thing Miss Flanagan prided herself on was that she kept a good table because, after all, 'an empty sack can't stand.'

The nun accepted and waved Alice forward, the first time she could ever remember sitting at the same table as the nun. She daintily nibbled on a ham sandwich while her new employer was told the story of how Alice had been abandoned as a baby on the steps of St Agnes's and had always been a model child.

'She's a biddable girl, says her prayers every night and morning and she's clean in all her habits.'

'I'm glad to hear it, she'll have to earn her keep here mind. I'm not as agile as I was and I wouldn't be going to this trouble only I need a young pair of hands and a strong back. If she's a slacker though, she'll go right back where she came from.' Miss Flanagan glared at the nun who hastened to reassure her.

'You'll not be disappointed. Alice has fine manners, is strong as an ox and I can promise you,' she repeated, 'she won't let you down.'

Miss Flanagan lifted the teapot again but Sister Margaret politely refused. After a few more pleasantries and reassurances, she went outside to where Thomas was waiting to drive her back to St Agnes's in the black car, sleek and shiny as a seal. That was the last Alice saw of her. Part of her was sad; the nun had always been kind to her, recognising her quickness in the school-room and singling her out when she sang in the choir at Mass.

Alice was already missing the other girls at St Agnes's, girls she'd grown up with and regarded almost as sisters, young women who'd shared her small joys and her sorrows whenever she'd felt sad. Bessie Ryan, her closest friend, promised to write to her and that if she herself got placed in work near her, maybe they could meet up. It all seemed vague and out of their reach but perhaps some day ...

Miss Flanagan's shop was perched on a bridge, under which a river journeyed to the sea. In some ways, Alice felt comforted by the sound of flowing water. Its constant presence over the following years lulled her to sleep and became the first thing she'd hear on waking in the attic room on the second floor up the rickety stairs from the shop.

Miss Flanagan soon realised that she had a treasure in Alice. She liked her company and sometimes, when Alice sang while working in the garden, she'd stop whatever she was doing just to listen to the pure, sweet sound. She often thought of the treasures that were given up by whoever it was abandoned the girl. But not knowing the circumstances, it wasn't her place to judge.

She was just glad that such a jewel had come her way. Thanks to Alice, the shop blossomed. Some of the land at the back of the shop was cleared. An abundance of flowers bloomed and vegetables sprouted for the table.

A small lean-to stored the coal. Shelves and glass-cases in the shop were polished and gleaming and Alice swept the floors and scrubbed the flagstones so that the whole place came alive again.

Over the years, salesmen all too often persuaded the old woman to buy goods that nobody wanted. Alice soon put a stop to all that. In the beginning when those salesmen arrived, or indeed customers, the colour sprang to her cheeks she was so shy with them. But now, three years later, she squared up to all with confidence. She also found out that her employer's name was Leonora but she was only ever referred to as Miss Flanagan, a mark of respect the old woman appreciated.

Bessie Ryan kept in touch as she'd promised, the two friends even managing to meet before Bessie eventually took the boat to America, finding work in a large department store in Boston. When Alice turned nineteen she reached a decision which shocked and frightened the old woman.

It was the middle of winter when the letter with the USA postmark reached the shop on the bridge. The river was swollen and the trees along the riverbank, trailed into the water, their branches heavy with rain. Miss Flanagan knew immediately that something not to her liking was coming when Alice asked her to sit down, that she had something to tell her.

'What is it girl?' she said in a cross voice. Although she had come to love Alice like a daughter, there was something hard within her that refused to soften outwardly. In some ways Alice was a reminder of what might have been had the love of her life, Pat Gleeson, not died prematurely from TB. 'Bad cess to him,' she often muttered. His memory still broke her heart.

'Is it that one over beyond?' she continued, referring to Bessie who had come to the shop once when passing through the town on her way to Dublin. Miss Flanagan had taken one look at Bessie's scarlet lipstick and dyed blonde hair before mentally dismissing her as inferior.

'Yes, it's Bessie,' Alice said in a faltering tone. She didn't often appear fidgety but her hands were clenched before her and she nervously shifted from one foot to the other.

'Well, out with it,' the old woman nearly barked. 'Is she in some trouble?' she then added, her blue eyes staring into Alice's startled ones. 'I always knew that one would come to no good; short skirts and high heels. Huh!' With that, Miss Flanagan sniffed and folded her arms across her chest.

'No, there's no trouble...' Alice said, almost tripping over the words. 'In fact, it's the opposite. Bessie is doing very well and has just been promoted to Manageress. She's asked me to join her in Boston. Bessie's got a heart of gold,' Alice continued in a rush. 'She's even sent me a ticket for the boat.' Alice took the letter and the ticket from her apron pocket for Miss Flanagan to see.

'Well, looks like your mind is made up then. Bad cess to you both. Who'll take care of the shop now? And me? I'm hardly able to walk some days with the rheumatism and the Lord knows what else ails me.' The truth was that she had been getting chest pains but wouldn't give in and go to the doctor whom she regarded as a quack and waste of money.

'Ah yes. Eaten bread soon forgotten. Was there ever a truer word?' Miss Flanagan felt a twinge of guilt when she saw the stricken look on Alice's face but she wouldn't relent. If she weakened now she would lose Alice for good and die a lonely old woman with no-one by her side when the final hour came. How often had she told Alice where the two candlesticks and white tablecloth were? All she wanted was to be laid out above the shop in the good sitting room where some of her kinder neighbours and customers might come and pay their respects.

'You know I'll have no-one if you go Alice,' she said, almost in a whisper, deciding to play her trump card. 'Me and you are alike Alice, all alone in the world, with neither kith nor kin. And besides, who'll run the shop when I'm gone? You know I have no-one to leave it to only yourself.'

There, she'd said it. The shop and all its contents had been willed to the Church long ago but it was all the old woman had to barter with. She could and would leave Alice the nest-egg under the floorboards in her bedroom, a tidy sum by any standard. She'd write a letter to Alice that very night, telling her where to find it, a letter not to be opened until after her death.

That night Alice barely slept, tossing and turning in her small bed under the eaves. Even the lullaby of the river couldn't soothe her. Bessie made everything seem so alluring. But if she stayed with Miss Flanagan, her future would be secure. Yet, there was a hankering deep within her for the life glimpsed in Bessie's letters, bright lights, gaiety and possibly romance. Yes, there would be hard work also but she'd never been afraid of that.

Then there was the old woman. She'd grown fond of her, knowing her bark was much worse than her bite and at the end of the day she'd taken her in. She had good food and a weekly wage. It wasn't a fortune but it covered her modest needs.

Alice decided to postpone her decision, a decision that delayed her trip to the New World by several months. In the end, it was Miss Flanagan herself who released her. One morning towards the end of January, when the surface of the river was skimmed with ice, the old woman failed to appear at her usual time to open the shop. Alice grew alarmed and went upstairs where nothing but silence answered her knocking.

Timidly, she opened the bedroom door. Miss Flanagan lay on her back, her face as snow white as the coverlet. Ebony Rosary beads were still wound around her fingers. Alice knew at once that the old woman had departed for the next life.

Tears gathered in her eyes as she bent to kiss the cold cheeks of the woman who had given her a home when all she'd ever known was the kindness of strangers. By her bedside was a letter addressed to Alice, a letter she put in her pocket before fetching the local doctor and the priest.

When the Will was read, Alice bore no grudge. Under the floorboards was enough money to ease her passage out into the wider world. Best of all, although Alice was more than a little heart-broken, she was starting out afresh, with a clear conscience and no regrets.

Eileen Casey lives in South Dublin but is originally from the Midlands. She has published a number of poetry and prose books (New Island, Arlen House) and was a Hennessy Award Winner (Emerging Fiction) in 2011. Her community press, Fiery Arrow, has been publishing writers in anthologies and in debut collections in recent years.